The Dogs On The Porch 3rd revision Copyright © July 2005

First Printing July 2005

Proudly printed in the U.S.A. by
    The Printer's Place
    8 South Fullerton Avenue
    Montclair, N.J. 07042   (973) 744-8889

Cover design
    The Stobb's Printing Company
    Bloomfield, N.J. 07003

ISBN 0-9650637-2-0

Lewis Wiyd

Dedications

To the Almighty for allowing me to live long enough to finish something that was more than fifty years in the making. To my wife Jan for her loving patience and fortitude. To Scooby and Train for being my rocks in the tossed seas of life. To my families where ever you may be. To Dusty, Jan, Johnni, Sharon, Melvon and Jackie for getting a too trusting and naiave guy past women's BS.

To Anna, Doris, Sharon H and Alicja. for their ears in allowing me to hear myself To BA/BMW it ain't no car and Sub-Group 166 1992 Columbia Md. for the focus. And to the Maree Family, for sharing a piece of their love.

Acknowledgments

Art Tolbert and family kindred spirits and artists.

The late Edward R. White Jr. for taking the time to care enough to help make it better.

Carol McGough for her critical assistance

Joseph P. Kennedy Esquire

Michael Baisden and The Love, Lust and Lies™ Radio show for verifying I ain't crazy.

How We Got Here (A brief history lesson)

History is often perceived as a series of linear events. But more often it is concurrent events in concert that affect major change. The best examples of these changes in Euro-American culture are technology and women's attitudes. And it was technology that greatly affected the change in the attitudes. In the eighteenth century most women couldn't own property. In fact many were property, indentured servants whose express purpose was to cook their husband's food, clean his house, and have his babies. Though there've always been laudable exceptions, generally most women fell into this traditional role.

Technology breeds technology, and nothing accelerates the process faster than war. Between World Wars One and Two there was a steady growth in time and labor saving devices coming into households. Each innovation freed more women from the time consuming drudgery and manual labor of running a household. The more free time they had, the more time they had to think about their plight. World War Two and the period following would spawn even faster innovation. But the war also did a great deal to plant the seeds of the Woman's Liberation Movement. For the first time, women left the home in vast numbers to do non-traditional jobs. After the war many of these women would never again be satisfied being strictly housewives. They planted the seeds of the feminist movement in their daughters by telling them stories about their adventures working in various industries. And it would be those daughters in the vanguard of the Lib movement twenty years later.

Another phenomenon of the war were the many hasty marriages by incompatible couples. The result of this was a major spike in the divorce rate after the war. But many women stayed in unsatisfying marital relationships for family and financial reasons. We'll now skip ahead to the decade of the sixties and the three additional factors that influenced many of the women's attitudes today.

The sixties may have been the decade that saw more social change than any prior decade in the history of the U.S.A. The feminist seeds had already been planted. In addition, the decade saw a major jump in the use of drugs, and the passage of the Civil Rights Act. But the thing that may have affected women's attitudes and behavior most was the introduction and wide spread use of the birth control pill. Prior to the pill many women remained chaste primarily due to the social stigma attached to unwed and teen pregnancy. The pill allowed women to cast aside chastity and begin to explore their sexuality freely.

Along with the drugs came Flower Power and the Hippie Free Love Movement, and this started a sexual revolution. At the time there was an unpopular war going on in Southeast Asia. Many veterans that weren't killed or maimed returned with severe emotional damage only to end up on drugs. The drug problem would eventually lead to the passage of what are known as the Rockefeller Drug Laws. And these laws would remove a lot of datable men from some minority communities. The result of this was slow and steady erosion of the traditional two parent family in that community. Even the government contributed to the erosion of the traditional family. Men unable to find employment were forced into estrangement from their families so the family could receive maximum public assistance benefits. And this brings us to the Civil Rights act of 1964.

The original intent of the law was to give minorities a chance to participate in areas where they'd been traditionally excluded. The law was later expanded to include gender, which allowed women to enter the work force in the largest numbers since World War Two. In truth the biggest beneficiary of the law were middle class white women. And they entered the work force with their new feminist attitudes. This attitude would eventually affect most of the women and men in the society. As we moved into the seventies women were exercising their new sexual freedom which resulted in the One Night Stand.

As more women became better educated, traveled and started businesses, many women in the minority community became overqualified to date the available men. This disparity in numbers caused a lot of men to become, as the old folks used to say, triflin'. Many of these women stopped holding men accountable and as a result too many men went from being gentlemen to players. This would further alter many women's attitudes yet again. The will to procreate in women is strong and many believed they could fill both parental roles equally well. And they began having children without any male father figures. The social stigma once attached to unwed pregnancy soon disappeared along with the traditional two parent family. This attitude would trickle down to teenage girls, and they began having babies.

Looking at this history leaves me both happy and sad. I'm happy for women's progress, and sad for what it's done for relationships and the traditional family. Fewer real fathers deny kids an opportunity to see examples of good relationship between a man and a woman. But women made this bed and now they have to sleep in it. You'll hear women say, "I don't need no man," and maybe they don't, but their kids do. Many of these women substitute their sons for relationships with mature men. This often turns the sons into Mama's Boys and cripples them for life. Too many young people are overfed, oversexed, and undereducated. Many have become slaves to peer pressure and music videos with lyrics that degrade and disrespect women. And that can't do much good for their future relationships. And it's the lyrics that bring me to my final point about the power of words and language.

Psycho-linguistics, or mind language, has become embedded into our culture in the form of political correctness. Nobody wants to offend anyone, and it's laudable, but it also creates a problem. The problem is societal ills never get fixed because we change the language to desensitize and make us feel better. Overweight peopled used to be fat and now they're big and that's acceptable, no matter how unhealthy they might be. Drunks and junkies became substance abusers, as the ghetto morphed into the inner city. The problems still exist but we don't see them because we changed the language. Language can also conjure romantic but unrealistic notions. For example- Someone to make me happy, or happily married, and falling in love are good examples of this. Happiness is a temporary state of mind, but what people really want is contentment. It's the comfortable middle ground between extreme joy and depression. Growing is always better than falling. And relationships that start with true friendships almost always last longer than those that start in some vague romantic notion of falling in love. And this brings me to my thoughts about good men.

About Good Men

I've heard a lot of women say over the years, *A good man is hard to find and all men are dogs.* The problem as I see it is not that good men are hard to find, but rather many women don't know what they want. They're so caught up in media generated images and bling bling, that many wouldn't know a good man if he bit her on the ass. This is particularly the case when they're younger. After life beats on them a bit, if they're lucky, they'll realize what they thought was important was actually trivial. I've taken the liberty to list some of the characteristics of a good man for those women that don't understand what I'm talking about. I won't elaborate, I'll just list them. A good man is:

Accountable
Compassionate
Communicative
Consistent
Friendly
Honest
Loving
Loyal
Patient
Reliable
Respectful
Spiritual
Supportive
Trustworthy
Understanding

Some of these characteristics are the very same ones that make some of us like dogs, the very dog women so often accuse us men of being. Perhaps it's time to find a better description than trying to compare men to dogs. As you can see, dogs have some very admirable qualities. Maybe men are more like bees, moving from flower to flower, and. that would definitely be a better comparison.

For all their ego driven macho bluster, men are emotionally more fragile than women. Because men are socialized to hold in their emotions they die earlier from complications of pent-up stress. When a man gets his heart broken, he's damaged goods. And he's likely to take his pain and frustration out on another innocent woman. Until or unless he resolves his issues, he can't successfully move into a successful relationship. This only exacerbates the problem as another disappointed woman buys into the *all men are dogs* mantra. If more women asked about unresolved issues before jumping in, they could avoid the pain and cynicism. But the truth is many women and men don't ask any questions at all before jumping into a relationship. And then sex gets involved and it becomes the focal point of the relationship. When the novelty of the sex wears off, there's nothing to sustain the relationship. It's no wonder over 50% of first marriages, and 75% of second marriages fail.

Apology;

I'd like to apologize to every woman that ever suffered any form of abuse from a man carrying baggage from unresolved emotional issues.

"Girlfriend, listen to me, All men are dogs"

"There has never been a divorce in the Rhymes Family."

Reason Benton Rhymes, Jr.

Fragile Men Creatures

Pigs and dogs they're called...
by those that don't understand
the pressures of being pulled constantly
in two directions

The first directions is pulled by friends
fearing they will think you weak
balancing on a bravado wire
showing the world a loose sand façade
protecting an eggshell

Reaching out with smiling tentativeness
with behaviors learned from the unlearned
Then being pulled... in the other direction by attraction
to soft round entities well practiced from birth
at wrapping daddy men around fingers

One day having that eggshell crushed...
while still having to walk that macho tightrope
A wounded an1mal reverts to behaviors learned
from the unlearned and now the ruthless
Thrusting spear at all soft round entities... for revenge

While eggshell becomes tempered steel
and caring is just a word... denoting pain
Then being labeled pig or dog
by self absorbed soft round entities
that don't care to understand and won't take the time to

while all the time still asking, where are all the good men

Lewis Wiyd

Why should anyone stand for anything
when we can simply fall for everything
why not do what's easy and expedient
let's just "go along and get along"
Nothing outrages us anymore
We've become sponges for acceptance
desensitized to the horrific and numb to the caring

Why strive for excellence when we can
Cop out, veg out, or sell out to mediocrity
We shouldn't 'rage into that good night',
because it's not the simple thing, it's not the popular thing
we'll just whimper into acceptance until nothing matters

Politicians became self servants, while same sex married
kids kill kids but that's alright,
it could never happen here
so let's make it legal, let's make it's okay
let's shove it down the throat of truth or tradition

And speaking of tradition

why not make a family one parent
let's make men and fathers obsolete
legal only as seed donors
devoid of any esteem, accountability or responsibility
After all, liberated dysfunction is politically correct

So why try and 'rage into that good night,'
when we can simply whimper into another acceptance
make it just, one more it's alright
just one more that's okay
until, that's alright and it's okay become nothing

And nothing matters only too nothing, if nothing is left

Chapter 1   Kickin' It

Hi, my name is Reason Benton Rhymes, Junior. My friends call me Reason B., but my family calls me Youngblood or Junior. You can call me anything you want except late for dinner as Grandpa would say. I'm twenty five years old and graduated Magna Cum Laude in the spring of 2001 from Virginia State University with a degree in business. But I didn't start school at Virginia State; I had an athletic scholarship for track at Villanova. At the end of my sophomore year, I tore up a knee and an Achilles tendon. The injury killed my dream of an attempt to make the U.S. Olympic Team. And when Villanova revoked my athletic scholarship, I transferred to Virginia State University.

College is the first experience many young people have to be on their own, and some go completely buck wild. Things were a lot different than when my folks were in college. The cell phone using, computer savvy, music video generation had different attitudes about almost everything, especially sex. And it was the young ladies that would have shocked my folks the most. Their in your face "What's up," approach was sometimes even shocking to me. And this was especially the case with some of the young women from less traditional families. State was very different from Villanova, and having been an athlete I'd lived a more regimented lifestyle. My roommate Jamal was a player, and I got an education walking in on him and some young co-ed. We hadn't seen each other in some time since graduation. And I left a day early on my way to the family reunion to hookup with him.

It was near noon when I got to his apartment. We'd planned to spend time catching up on things. I was gonna spend the night and leave from his place and go on to the reunion. Jamal was a computer nerd, without the nerd part. And as I said before he was a player. He'd landed a good job with a Fortune 500 company and was doing quite well. We went out for lunch, and he started flirting with the waitress. We had a good time talking and laughing about our college days. As we were leaving the diner the waitress slipped him her number and told him to call her. It was obvious that though Jamal had joined the real world he was still up to his old tricks. That night I'd find out just how hard old habits were to break, and there would also be a shocking surprise.

I had no intention of going out that night, but Jamal talked me into it telling me he had a surprise for me. We went to a very popular watering holes arriving about ten. The place was packed and the women outnumbered the men by about five to one. I was a little uncomfortable by all the attention, but Jamal was right in his element. He was going through the crowd looking for someone. Suddenly I spotted Chacita, Jamal's old college girlfriend. When she saw him she walked into his arms and put her arms around his neck and kissed him. I watched as she practically rammed her tongue down his throat. It was an obvious action to show the women that this man belonged to her. As I watched, someone stepped up beside me and slipped an arm through mine. Turning to see who it was, my eyes landed on the pretty face and large light brown eyes of one Dalita Ann Watson.

"Waz up Lita, it's great to see you again, I said smiling at her. "It's great to see you again too Reason," she said as she leaned over and kissed me on the cheek. Lita was tall, and in heels we stood eye to eye. But the thing that had caused most of her problems in college was her body. Voluptuous would have been the way to describe her, and she was built like the proverbial brick out house. Almost every straight guy at State was trying to get into her pants. She came from a strict and rather sheltered home, and was one of those co-eds that went buck wild when she first got to State. Chacita had befriended her and pulled her coat to the real deal about guys and they'd become best friends. Lita loved to dance and was a dancer with the marching band. I'm not much of a drinker, but we all had quite a bit that night, as we talked, laughed and danced up a storm. We left around midnight and they followed us back to Jamal's apartment.

Chacita and Dalita were that new breed of woman my mom called *Femen*. These women didn't feel compelled to adhere to the traditional roles or values of women. My mom explained this frightens many men because these women couldn't be easily controlled through emotional attachments. They couldn't be abused or disrespected because they weren't emotionally attached. In some respects they were more like men, and could easily separate their sexuality from their emotions. She said this attitude developed because of the shortage of men. Many women had been hurt and disappointed so often by men abusing their emotions; they developed the attitude to protect their feelings. They detested the societal double standards for men and women. But the thing they detested more, was being judged, labeled, or boxed by that standard. And their attitude was anyone that didn't understand or couldn't deal with their free spirited attitude, could go to hell. The members of the Rhymes Family stressed the importance of being honest, and gender equality. Male children were treated the same as the girls, even having the same curfews. It was also well established if you cheated on a Rhymes woman, she had the right to cheat on you.

I never understood the relationship between Chacita and Jamal, but it wasn't my place to understand it. As long as it worked for them it was cool. He'd once explained they had an open relationship, and as long as their actions didn't land on the other's doorstep, what they did, and with whom was their own business. When we got to Jamal's place he and Chacita went straight into his bedroom and closed the door, leaving Lita and me sitting on his sofa alone. Like most guys I'd always had an attraction to her. But I may have been one of the few guys at school who trying to screw her. As a result of our respective relationships with Jamal and Chacita, we were around each other quite a bit. We got to know each other through our conversations. And she always sought me out when she needed someone to talk to. Now we were sitting on the sofa and things were awkward and tense. She suddenly sat in my lap, put her arms around my neck and kissed me.

She'd been a virgin when she'd arrived at State, and rumor had it she'd fulfilled more than her academic education. But she always maintained a ladylike demeanor, and since guys tended to exaggerate when it came to sex, I thought nothing of it. Our relationship had been plutonic, but there was always a sexual tension between us. It may have been something we'd always wanted to do, or perhaps we'd consumed enough alcohol for our inhibitions to all but disappear. But whatever it was, we wound up going at each other with an animalistic lust. It turned out that the rumors were true, as my manhood seemed glued in her mouth most of the night, and I couldn't tell which of us was enjoying it more. My sexual education was completed that night when she backed it up and I liked it so much I went back for a second helping. We fell asleep somewhere in the wee hours of the morning cuddled together.

It was near ten the next morning when I awoke and went to take a shower. Everyone else got up shortly after that, and I knew I'd been set up when Lita sent me out to her car to bring in their overnight bags from the trunk. I fixed us all breakfast and the girls left shortly afterward. Before they left Lita made me promise I'd call her and keep in touch. And she knew if I gave my word I'd keep it. After they'd gone Jamal and I talked and laughed awhile longer until it was time for me to leave to continue on to the reunion. The whole trip to Grandpa's farm I thought about the best sexual experience of my life with Lita.

I'd always been conflicted when it came to having casual sex. I'd been raised to believe you had to be in a relationship with a woman before you engaged. But sometimes the flesh got weak like it had with Lita. And I was feeling guilty that I'd given into my lustful desire. I'd wanted to be with her since the first time I'd seen that voluptuous hour glass figure. And I suppose I was more upset with myself that I'd given into it. But I couldn't have known at the time I'd see a lot more of her when a promotion transferred her into my area. And we'd eventually become best friends in a nonsexual relationship. As I drove I also thought about the reunion and growing up in the Rhymes Family.

Chapter 2

Rhymes, Love, Kids, Wisdom and Song

The transfer to State made the Rhymes family happy for two reasons. First it was closer to home and the second, and more important, was the Rhymes family was a Virginia State U. family. Almost everybody in the family went there. The only exception was Grandpa Wisdom and Grandma Essence. They didn't attend college, but if you saw their library you'd understand that they didn't need to. My Grandparents have read a lot of the books in there. Before there was a public library, the Rhyme's Family library was it, complete with Dewey Decimal System.

From the time the Rhymes Kids were old enough to start elementary school we spent our summer vacations on Grandpa's farm down south. There were always four or five grandchildren on the farm in the summer. At the end of every day after supper we would sit out on the front porch and Grandpa or Grandma would read to us. Getting a gift for the Grandparents is never a problem, you just bring a book.

Sometimes they'd tell us stories. These stories always had a moral in them. Other times we'd get a sort of history lesson about the Family. These were always a special treat for me. That's how I first found out about my Great Great Great Grandfather Israel Wisdom Rhymes. Family lore has it he invented the Cotton Gin that Eli Whitney is generally given credit for. And, he was one of the freed slaves that actually got the forty acres and a mule, though how he got the mule is left to some question.

I must have been about ten and my Sister Common Sense, whose given name is Carmen Ennis, was maybe thirteen. As usual, we were sitting on the porch after dinner. Grandma Essence (whose given name is Essie Henchel) was telling us about members of the family. After reciting a long list of the family tree, she told us there hadn't ever been a divorce in the Rhymes family. She then said she expected us to keep this tradition going. I was amazed Grandma could remember so many names, dates and places. This was the first of many times Grandma amazed me.

When I was young I thought Grandpa was the smartest man I'd ever met. The only person I thought was smarter was Grandma, because he always did whatever she asked. I once asked him if I'd ever be as smart as he is, and he said what he didn't know, would make two new worlds. He told me I should try to learn something new everyday, quoting, "The most blessed thing about learning is mistakes are expected, and accepted." As I grew up I began to understand my perception of their relationship had nothing to do with intelligence. It was based on mutual respect, trust, friendship, and a deep love. Speaking of love, anyone who ever spent any time around the Rhymes Family would never have a doubt they are loved. The reason is you are hugged and told you are loved as often as possible.

Now I don't want give anyone the impression that the Rhymes Family is perfect. We've black sheep in the family like every other family. But as far as I know, we've never had anyone do anything bad enough to go to jail. If the children do something out of line, they are corrected by any adult that happens to be present. If they do something to warrant a belt or switch, that's what they get. It's not abuse, its discipline, and that's all it is. Like I said, we never had anyone do anything bad enough to go to jail. Grandpa always says, "Spare the rod, and ruin the child". There's no 'Time Out,' or go to your room and think about what you've done wrong. It was the belt or the switch, and you immediately knew what you did bad enough to warrant the pain, and don't do it again.

In all the summers that I spent on the farm he only whipped me once. He told me not to do something and I did it anyway. Grandma also whipped me once for the same reason. Only hers were worse because she had me go get the switch she was going to whip me with. That wily old lady could teach a psychology professor something about psychology.

My grandparents are always talking about setting a good example for children. They say, "People always learn more from what they see, than from what they hear." The way they say it is, "Do what you see, and see what you do." They are always talking about parenting consistency with a phrase they learned from Great Grandpa, "What one does, all does." These phrases have become a part of me, and have shaped many of my attitudes.

My grandparents always said if you associate with people of good character you will have good character. As they put it, "Birds of a feather flock together and snakes travel with snakes." They say, "If you choose to sleep with dogs, you must be prepared to wake up with fleas." Every action has a consequence, and you must consider your actions carefully. There's a word you are not allowed to use in the Family. That word is can't. Whenever anyone uses the word, you will hear a chorus of, "Can't never tried." You don't know if you can't do something unless you try. Grandma always says, 'Every opportunity to try something new, it's an opportunity to learn something new, and you learn more from the mistakes."

I already told you that my grandparents are smart. They are to the community what America Online is to the Internet, collectors and dispensers of information and knowledge. It's born out by the fact that folks are always dropping by to talk. They usually come at meal time. During our summers on the farm, we saw all kinds of people drop by the house to seek advice from our grandparents. Sometimes strangers would stop by asking for advice. Some of these folks we knew, and some were complete strangers. Since these folks usually came at a meal time, Grandma would invite them to eat. She says, "Never trust anyone who won't share a meal with you."

These folks would stop for advice or to just borrow something. At times they just came to chew the fat and socialize. I once said to Grandpa that everybody liked him. He replied not everyone liked him, but rather they had respect for him. He then said, "If you respect yourself, others will respect you."

My grandparents are like two peas in a pod. They're one third compassion, one third common sense and one third cunning. And, they have a huge measure of humor thrown in for good measure. Like I said, folks would drop by for advice. However, I never actually heard them give any. They would listen, nod now and then, say a word here or there but you would never hear them speak a whole sentence. One day I asked Grandma how she could give a person advice if she never said anything. Her answer was so simple that it amazed me.

"Most of the time, people don't want advice. They pretty much already know what they need to do. They just need someone to listen so they can hear it out loud." Now if a person was about to do something that to their way of thinking is going end with negative results, they never say "I wouldn't do that if l were you". Instead they'd ask, "Are you sure that's what you want to do?" Then they would have the person go down the list of options again. By the time the person left, they'd have picked the best option without my grandparents actually telling them what to do. They never talk to anyone else about other people's problems or business. Well, they do talk to each other naturally, but they don't carry tales as the old folks used to say. They say, "If you keep what people tell you, they will tell you everything." I also always heard, "Don't tell folks all you know, because then they will know what they know and all that you know."

Grandma says, "Bought sense is the best sense" which means you learn by paying for your mistakes. She also says, "Don't judge your worth by what you can buy." Grandma's always coming out with these tidbits of wisdom. When she thought I was ready to learn about sex, she sat me down and taught me the facts. Using examples of the farm animals, it was done with such skill that I didn't feel any great urge to go out and try it. She answered all my questions, and by the time we were done she gave me a sort of test to make sure I understood. I figure when or if I ever have kids, I'm going to have Grandma tell my kids too.

After this, she began adding new wisdom I'd never heard before. They included; "Never beat your woman because you can't sleep with one eye open", or "Never marry a woman that keeps a dirty house because if she won't take care of her house, she won't take care of you," and then there's the one that goes, "A woman can look up longer than you can look down." All while I was growing up and to this day, my dad will bring flowers or candy or something to my mother from time to time. I now know this is directly attributable to that little tidbit of wisdom that goes, "The same thing it takes to get a woman, it takes to keep her." I used to hear Grandma say all the time, "If you don't look for love, it will find you." Then she'd add, "Seek friendship first, and love will follow."

One day she said to me that men and women often wanted the same things out of life, "That the need to be needed was the primary need." Then she said, "There are three things a man wanted from a woman: they want a lady in the street, a mother in the home and a whore in the bed." Also she said the three things a woman wanted from a man were, "A gentleman in the street, a father in the home and a bull in the bed." It was at this time I was having my first teenage crush and I thought I was in love.

As usual I left home for my summer on the farm. Needless to say, by the time I returned home that summer, the young lady had a new boyfriend and I was devastated. I'd always heard that 'Absence makes the heart grow fonder.' But this obviously couldn't be right because in my absence this young lady's heart had forgotten me. I eventually got over it, and she wasn't replaced by another girl, but by track and field. This led to my athletic scholarship to Villanova.

My Grandparents are always saying that, "The only constant in life is change." They say if you lock your mind on one point of view, you close yourself off to all the other possibilities. "Change is like a train going down the track of life. You can get on board, or get left behind. You might not like it, but you'd better understand it." I always heard that despite all the changes that life will bring, "The ultimate goal in life is inner happiness if you seek this first, all else will follow."

I remember one summer I had arrived on the farm, and done my usual walk around to see the changes (there was always something new), I went into the library and sitting on the desk was a computer. I hurried into the kitchen to ask Grandma who it was for. She said she and Grandpa were learning how to use it. They already knew this machine was going to change the world. Then she started singing as she prepared dinner. Singing is one of the two constants in the family. Grandpa came into the kitchen spouting verses in rhythmic patterns, which is the other constant He added his bass to Grandma's alto as they sang, in perfect harmony while smiling at each other.

The Sounds of Music

One of the constants in the Rhymes Family, which is as sure as the sun rising in the east, is music. Everyone in the family is either singing, playing, or listening to some form of music. It's as if a day would not be complete if there wasn't any music in it. During my summers on the farm my grandparents were constantly singing while doing the many and varied tasks required to run a farm. We'd do call and response in the fields, or classic pop and rhythm and blues in the barn and tobacco lofts. The one thing I'm always certain of is there will be music. Growing up if my grandparents weren't reading or telling us stories, they'd be singing to us. Anytime they had a spare moment you might find them in the living room listening to records or the radio. We grew up with all kinds of music. It ranged from gospel to opera, and everything in between. It's impossible to attend a family gathering of any kind without the singing together. They always say, "Music is a universal language." There's no better example of this than what happens at a family reunion.

On the Saturday afternoon of the reunion, everyone gathers on the front porch to sing. Many years ago some neighbors stopped by during the family sing and they joined in. Now it has become a tradition that much of the community comes to the Rhymes Family Sing. It's not unusual to count two hundred or more people on and around that porch. They bring lawn chairs and cakes, pies and lemonade. During the Sing people will leave the singing from time to time and go have cake or pie and then rejoin the group. This event usually lasts for about two to three hours. Then, just like that, all the neighbors slowly start to leave until just the family is left.

I guess you could say the only time I was taken back by a type of music was the time I caught my grandparents listening to Hip Hop. When I asked them about it, they said they wanted to know what the attraction was for the young folks. Grandpa says that some distant relative of the family could have invented this form of music. He says this because there is another trait common in the family. And that is that many of the family members are wordsmiths or poets.

Rhymes' Rhymes

If ever a family had a surname that was appropriate, it would be the Rhymes Family. Just as you will always hear music and singing in the family you are likely to hear someone reciting verses of some form or other. As far back as I can remember, I have heard family members reciting verses. It's a thing that just seems to run in the Rhymes Family Genes. I first realized that I had it at six years old when I wrote my first verse. My mother still has those words in a frame on her bedroom wall.

Lewis Wiyd

"I like mommy, and mommy likes me, I'm talking about the mommy on my family tree.

She's not very old, and she's not very young, but she's still my mommy, and she's sure some chum."

You can never tell where the inspiration will come from. They seem to spring from any occurrence or even a word. All I know is it seems to pop up out of nowhere. They take many forms, from rhyme to one line thoughts. These poems actually have a prominent place as one of the events at the family reunions which I call Word Wars.

Who Knows on what fickled wings doth fly, the seeds of creation's flight That compels the song writer to put down notes, or the verses poets write.

Word Wars usually take place after the family circle, (I'll explain this later), and the evening meal. I've made a habit of taping the Word Wars from the time I was a sophomore in high school. When ever I have some free time I usually type them up, make copies and distribute them at the next family function. For me, they are one of the highlights of the family reunion. It usually starts on the front porch with someone reciting a piece. From there it takes on a life of its' own and can head in any direction as each of the participants jumps in with their piece. It can last anywhere from forty five minutes to an hour and a half And on rare occasions I've heard them go for as long as three hours. Word Wars usually end when Grandpa or Grandma get up to go into the house. We all then just sit on the porch and listen to the crickets and watch the stars, laugh and talk.

Family Reunion

The Third Sunday in August is one of the traditional times for southern homecomings and reunions. I don't know how it got to be this way, but that's the way it is. You just mark the date on your calendar and plan to attend. A large number of the family shows up for the reunion. And those that can't attend will be thinking about it wherever they may be. Some of the folks will start to trickle in on the Friday before, but almost everybody arrives by late Saturday morning. As I've already said, it takes about an hour to get through the hugs and I love yous. Then folks settle into small groups to catch up on things that are going on in the various family groups.

Somewhere around noon the picnic will begin out in the back yard. Every body brings a dish of something. All the while there's the constant sound of talk and laughter with kids running everywhere. The picnic begins when Grandpa Wisdom says a prayer followed by, "Let's eat." After the meal folks mill around or go for walks around the farm to see what changes have taken place. Others will go out to the cars and take a nap or play cards until it's time for the family sing, which I already told you about.

At the end of family sing, the folks mill around and talk and laugh some more until it's time for the Family Circle. This is the event where everyone sits in a large circle. It starts with Grandma Essence saying a prayer. Everyone says their name and gives a brief description of the things currently occurring in their lives. After this, Grandma Essence goes down that long family tree list. She says a prayer for any of the family members that might have passed on during the year. You always know when the Family Circle has ended because Grandma will say, "And thank God there has still never been a divorce in the Rhymes family." Everyone applauds, and heads off for the evening meal. This is more of a pot luck type of meal. You usually end up eating more of the same things that you ate at the picnic. The other thing is it's not a sit down meal. Grandpa says a prayer and you get your plate and find a seat anywhere you can. After this, Word Wars begins which I've already mentioned. And on Sunday everyone goes to church.

The church is usually packed because of all the reunions in the area. After the morning service everyone has lunch. After lunch the afternoon service begins. Those that have a long way to travel usually leave to return home. Folks staying in the area are encouraged to attend revival. Revival is a week long event which is held in the church every night of the week. They have guest speakers and choirs for each service. Since Grandpa is a deacon, if you are on vacation you will go to Revival. I guess that's about all I can tell you about the family reunion. Now I'm going to tell you about a personal experience that happened at that reunion.

Chapter 3

The Dogs on the Porch

"What I'm about to tell you now is strictly from hind sight. When it happened to me, I never knew it was deeply rooted in tradition. Over the years I had been an unwitting participant in diversions to keep the children occupied in games and farm tours while this event took place on the front porch. Now it was happening to me, and I was totally unaware. Every member of the Rhymes family, or any person that marries into the family, goes through the process. I'm now convinced they didn't know any better than I did that it was happening to them during the actual process. In fact, I never caught on until after I'd gotten home from the reunion and my Mom called me, but I'll tell you more about this later.

It's the women that determine when a young man is mature enough for the process, and it's time to put the dogs on the porch. It started innocently enough in the summer after my junior year at State and I was doing a summer internship. I came home one day and Mom and Aunt Ester (Uncle Question's Wife) were sitting in the kitchen. They both looked up when I came in and spoke. Then Aunt Ester said to Mom, "I think it's time to put the dogs on the porch." Mom just said, "I think you may be right." Now, I'm a curious person and this didn't make sense to me so naturally I asked what they meant. (We had a dog, she'd died, and we never got another one.) Mom just said, "You'll find out," then they started talking about something else. I didn't think anymore about it, and fixed a snack and left. Because of the internship I wasn't able to make the family reunion the next two years, so the event was postponed until after graduation.

Now I've already mentioned that my grandparents are cunning, and Grandma Essence is as cunning as they get. She could sell a drowning man a glass of water and make him think he was doing her a favor by buying it. Anyway, from the time I was about sixteen or so, no matter what event or family gathering we attended she would manage to get me alone for five minutes to talk to me. These sessions weren't anything like the talks we usually had. They were different because I'd be doing all the talking. She has the sweetest way of getting you to tell her everything and you don't realize you're doing it. That's how she found out I was no longer a virgin. I now know these talks were maturity evaluations.

Mom had been reminding me for months about the upcoming reunion. Even Dad mentioned it a couple of times. As the date got closer she would say, "We'll be leaving for the farm on Friday, the day before the main events." I didn't think this was unusual because we'd done it before. I left a day early to see my old college roommate Jamal, whom I hadn't seen in over a year. I met my family at the farm on Friday afternoon. I greeted everyone and then went on my usual tour to see what changes had taken place. At dinnertime we all sat down to eat in the dining room Other than there seemed to be more people there on a Friday than usual, I didn't think anything was out of the ordinary.

After dinner I took my plate into the kitchen and went out on the porch. Shortly after that, Dad came out, followed shortly after by Grandpa and Uncle Question. Grandpa put his corncob pipe in his mouth. Grandpa always had that pipe. Even though he grew tobacco, he didn't smoke. He just put that pipe in his mouth and chewed on it. We all started talking and they asked me questions about what I was planning to do now that I had graduated and had a job.

I should have suspected something was up because we'd been sitting on that porch for a few minutes and I hadn't seen hide nor hair of a woman or child, and you can't go to any kind of Rhymes family function without seeing a woman or child every few minutes. But there's something about a beautiful southern summer evening and a full belly that tends to dull the senses. So I didn't suspect anything because I was enjoying the moment.

Grandpa broke the silence when he said, "Junior, now that you're out of school and you have a job, have you got any prospects?" I asked what he meant. He said, "You know, women prospects. Is there a special lady in your life?" I told him, "No." Then I said, "I have been so busy learning the job and furnishing my new apartment that I've barely had time to sleep, much less date." Grandpa then asked what it I was looking for in a woman. After thinking about it for a second I said, "I really don't know. I guess I want someone who wants the same things I want." Then Dad asked "What is it that you want?" I had thought about this on occasion and at this point in my life I wasn't sure. So I said, "Well I'd like to get my career off the ground and eventually start my own business like you and Uncle Question. I'd like to meet an incredibly intelligent and beautiful woman and eventually settle down and have a family." That's when Uncle Question asked how I planned to meet this woman? I thought about this for second and I realized that I really didn't have the slightest idea how I was going to pull off the most important decision of my life. So I said, "I have no idea." That's when he said, "My boy, let me tell you a little story."

Wooof!

Suddenly, everyone was drawn by the sound of someone walking on the sidewalk about forty feet nom the porch. All heads turned in unison in the direction of the sound. It was Mrs. Dixson's youngest daughter Zelda. She was a curvy young lady of about sixteen. She had on a faded pair of tight fitting jeans and a halter top. When she was in front of the walkway she smiled, waved, and spoke to Grandpa. "How you doin' this evenin Mr. Rhymes?" We all smiled and spoke in unison as she continued on up the sidewalk. But nobody's eyes moved away from that rhythmic sway of her hips and buttock as she walked up the sidewalk until she was out of sight. Then Dad said "That young lady sure has a body on her." And the rest of us nodded in agreement. I then said, "I could fall in love with a body like that." There was a moment of silence and Uncle Question began to recite...

Now fellas here's a warning,
some wisdom you should heed.
I know it's only natural,
when fighting mongrel breed.
You gotta know the difference
from what you feel, and what you see.
To make it even plainer,
know what you want, and what you need.
Don't fall in love with no bodies,
is what I'm here to say.
For ravages of time and gravity,
those bodies take away.
Don't ever be a victim to,
lustful visions of the eyes
Those curves are oh so tempting,

Lewis Wiyd

in tight sweaters,
and skirts revealing thighs
But if you love a body,
it's sure to fade with time.
Be sure to never give your love,
til you know what's in her heart.
Those curves are oh so tempting
but you gotta be about much more.
Make sure she's got some substance,
before hanging hat inside her door.
Don't fall in love with no bodies,
relationships need more than that,
and there'd better be a whole lot more,
when tempting curves have turned to fat.

Chapter 4

Mistakes and Questions

Uncle Question (whose given name is Quinton Eston) is my Dad's younger brother. He is also the youngest child of my grandparent's five children. He had special talents and my grandparents sent him to live with Grandpa's brother in the city so he could attend a special school. From the time he was twelve he lived in the city. Everyone always says he was late in developing while growing up. In fact, they say he didn't lose his last baby tooth until he was fifteen. He got married when he was in his thirties, so I guess he must have dated for quite a while. Though I hate to admit it, he's my favorite uncle because he always took me fishing when I was growing up. He never treated me like a child but rather as a young adult. Now here we were sitting on Grandpa's front porch and he began telling us this story.

"To start with this young man was what some people would call a hopeless romantic. He believed in the old ways, but the woman's liberation movement had taken a lot of fun out of dating. In addition, the conspicuous consumption eighties generation made it extremely difficult for good men to survive in the wars of romance. Believe me, it was a war which was sad, because to him it was something that should've been fun. Instead it had turned into a hassle and a battle of wills and will nots. To quote Sista Souljah...

"The reason men and women have so many problems in relationships, is because men don't do what they say and women have hidden agendas."

"From his perspective, women's hidden agendas was the reason he had problems with them. Now, how many times have you seen women in relationships who believe they can change their men? If there's something that they don't like about the man they feel if they love him enough they can change what they don't like. In truth, the only person that can change a person is the person themselves. If a person is unable or unwilling to change, no other person can make them do it. But I've digressed, so let's get on with it.

This boy spent his summers with his parents. They were wonderful people blessed with patience and wisdom. He was had a loving family and great support. He was also blessed to be surrounded by strong women and positive male role models. He grew up in a community where everyone watched out for all the children. He was raised in the Christian family values. He was taught manners and respect for others and their property. As he grew up he did the things that most boys of the era did, like sports and the Boy Scouts. Though he didn't know it at the time he grew up in a very sheltered environment. And this later caused him many problems. He spent a couple of weeks in the summer on vacation with his Uncle's family, usually at the beach. Because of this he developed a love for the ocean which is why he'd later join the Navy.

Like most boys, one day he discovered girls. And he had the normal curiosity about those wonderful different creatures. During high school he had a sweetheart and did what was in those days the normal daring thing. He labored under many false assumptions about the so-called gentle gender. And it was these falsehoods that further caused problems in his development of a meaningful and lasting relationship.

When he was younger, what he was looking for in a woman was an unattainable set of requirements. You might find some of these things in one person, but you'd better believe not all these things could be found in one person. I guess what he was looking for in a woman was perfection. He was terribly naive in thinking he could find all this in one woman. He was looking for a woman like his grandmother and his mother. This was the last generation of super women who had many skills, jobs and took care of their families without the helpful conveniences found today. He never heard them complain about how unfair life was."

Women are Smarter than Men

"When it came to relationships he was convinced that women were smarter than men. He could never figure out why when he was dealing with them he always seemed to be one step behind in their thought process. It was as if they had a crystal ball and could predict what he was going to do before he did it. Was it because of some sixth sense they had? Or could it be that he might have been too predictable? The answer came much later for him. And it was not as complicated as he first suspected."

Misguided Respect

"Since he'd been reared around strong positive women, he might have developed a misguided outlook about all other women. He probably developed more of a respect than he should have. This may have contributed to some of the problems he had later with the gentler sex. Because everything is a learning experience, he eventually learned what he really wanted. All this learning came at great cost in time, aggravation and expense.

The women he grew up around were honest with him. This may have been the only disservice they paid to him. For it led to a mistaken belief that all women were honest. Nothing could be further from the truth. Women are human, and like all humanity some are honest and some are not. With so many fewer eligible men available now than years ago this problem is getting worse. This perceived man shortage may be causing some women now to be less than truthful with men than they might otherwise be. When lies beget lies nobody benefits.

For some reason, this lesson was the hardest to learn and it took our man the most time, for he tried to be an honorable person. When you try to be an honorable person and you've associated with honorable people, your view of the world tends to be that it is an honorable place. Now I know you are saying this guy was a sap, and he should have known better, but what could he say, it was the way he was raised."

The First Mistake

"The first mistake a lot of men make regarding women is listening to other men. The truth is, most probably don't know anymore about them than you do. And, there are a lot of men who tend to be very liberal with reality when discussing their exploits with women. In order to avoid this mistake, you'd be better served by getting information you need from women. However, I'd caution you that it might be wise to have some kind of relationship with any women you choose to ask the important questions. The reason is you don't want them to get the wrong idea as to why your asking."

Asking Questions

After a pause Grandpa said, "In my day we made a lot more assumptions. But given the changes in attitudes and society, it's not wise to make those assumptions today. When we do business with people, we have no problem asking questions. We ask about their track record and what's expected of us. And we tell them what our expectations are of them. But when people are about to get into a relationship, often they don't ask anything at all. Too often they're already in the relationship before they discover things they can't accept. By then feelings have gotten involved and it can turn into a real mess. Much of this could have been avoided if they'd simply asked some questions before it started. There's a good chance they'd never have gotten involved at all had they asked the questions in the beginning."

Then Dad said, "I think the reason people don't ask questions is because they think people will think they're being nosey. But if there's a possibility emotions could get involved, it's very important the questions be asked. And you've got to be willing to be honest and answer any question you ask. People tend to be on their best behavior when they first meet someone. And often you can't see traits that might be unacceptable to you. It's very disappointing to find yourself in an unpleasant situation after something happens. If you ask the questions then, it seems even worse when they say the reason they didn't tell you was because you never asked. The worst thing people can't do to each other is waste each other's time. And if you don't ask the questions, that's really what you're doing."

Then Uncle Question said, "Junior you're living in a different era than we dated in. It's more important than ever to ask questions now-a-days. The questions should be asked in the initial stage of dating, some maybe even the first date.

And it shouldn't be an inquisition, but in the normal course of conversation. You need to know if a woman has had a same sex relationship We're living in the era of the down-low, so sexual orientation should be one of the initial questions. I know from my own personal experience this assumption can be especially emotionally damaging. The next question should be about the current status of her relationship.

Often people might be married or in a relationship and looking for a little something on the side. If the person isn't in a relationship, it's important to know when they were in their last serious one. You should know how long the relationship lasted and why it ended. Sometimes the relationship is supposedly over but booty calls are still being made. Then there's the woman that might have been relationship that's over but the former interest is unstable, jealous and stalking her. These are things you need to know before getting involved, because her problems are your problems if you do.

You're also living in an era where sex kills. And you'd be wise to ask about this too. I know it sounds cold, but before you engage sexually you might even ask to see a recent test result. And ask if they've had sex since they've had the test. And while we're talking about sex, before you get serious you need to know if they have any molestation or rape issues they haven't resolved. About one in three women have been molested, and about one in six has been raped. These experiences can leave very deep emotional scars. And before you get serious about a woman you need to know if she's carrying baggage from these or any other abuse issues. After you've determined the relationship status, it's important to know about her relationship with a father figure."

Then Grandpa said, "We're living in the era of the liberated woman with many young people coming from non-traditional homes. It's important for a young man like you to know about a woman's relationship with her father. Women that grow up in good relationships with their fathers or father figures tend to be less confrontational. They learn early how to deal with a man and know when to pick their battles. They're less likely to want to go toe-to-toe with you on every issue, and they've learn how to compromise. They also know instinctively what intimacy with a man is like in a non-sexual way. And they can submit to letting a man be himself without taking it as a personal affront to their womanhood."

Then Uncle Question said, "Women and men can be friends. In fact, they can be the best of friends as long as they follow one rule. They should never go to bed together because as soon as this happens the relationship will change. Now I'm going to contradict myself and say that a wife should be a best friend. But you need to know that there should be a discussion to change their friendship to something else before they alter the relationship. But again I'm getting ahead of myself so we'll talk more about this later.

Anyway, the reason men and women have difficulty maintaining a friendship after they go to bed together is because men tend to separate their hearts from their bodies, and many women don't. Mind you, this is not a fault, but a part of the socialization process. Of all the things he learned about women on the long road to the Alter, this was the hardest lesson for him to learn. And it took a group of women friends (The Committee) to explain it to him. We'll talk more later about this too.

The Second Mistake

"The second mistake many men make is confusing love and lust. I wouldn't begin to claim to be an expert as to the reasons this happens, but I can tell the difference. There is an easy test a man can give himself that will give a good indication as to which he is dealing with. The test is simple; you ask yourself what you thought about the first time you saw the woman. If the only thing you could think of was taking her to bed, it's lust. If, on the other hand, you said to yourself you'd like to get to know what kind of person she was, then there's a possibility for love. The reason I say possibility, is because if you take the time to get to know her you might discover that you can't stand her. To emphasize the positive side of the point, I'd like to relate what happened to a friend of mine.

When he met his wife he worked for a company repairing typewriters, and he was in her office doing a repair. He said that upon meeting her he knew that this was the woman he was going to marry. To make a long story short, it's over thirty years later and they're still married. I asked him what the first thought he had after meeting this women was, and he said that he wanted to know her better. I then asked him if the thought of going to bed entered his head and his answer was no. I don't want you to think people can't have a physical attraction and then fall love, because the truth is most often the first attraction is physical. I'm only saying that there is a difference in the thought process between lust and potential love.

Chapter 5

Uncle Question Tells a Story
First Love, Forever love

"Junior, I want to tell you a story about a young man and the very first person he fell in love with. Think past the puppy love and on to that first raging passionate feeling that affects you in ways for which you are forever changed. For him that first love was so profound that it shadowed him all way to marriage. In fact, he had to first exorcise the demons of that relationship before he could get married."

How They Met

"In this Information age with all the computers, fax machines and Cell-phones, it seems strange that he met Love the old fashion way, she wrote him a letter. He was in Vietnam at the time and a relative she worked with asked her if she'd send him a letter to boost his morale. She sent the letter and that started a steady flow of letters both ways. They wrote each other for about two months. Finally, he asked her what she looked like and she sent him a description including the usual things: height, weight, etc. When he got to the part about green eyes, he was blown away and they've been his weakness ever since. She also sent a picture which blew him away. When he thought about her his first thought was about the beautiful green eyes. Beautiful eyes were his weakness, and this was before the age of colored contact lenses.

When he got home from Vietnam the first thing he did was go to her job to say hello. He went into the bank, and after saying hello to his relative, he was introduced to her.

After meeting her he knew he had met the woman of his dreams. She was the most beautiful woman he had ever seen. He later thought to himself that if he had not been through so many near death experiences he would never have spoken to her. As far as women were concerned he was kind of awkward. Like a lot of young men, he didn't deal with rejection very well. It was Tuesday and they made a date for Friday night. When he left the bank the first thing he did was to go down the Street to buy a car. He went to the VW dealership and he bought a red Karmann Ghia. Now he was ready! He had a date with the world's most beautiful woman, and he had a car. Come on Friday night.

I shouldn't have to tell you but from Tuesday 'til Friday all he could think about was the date with this woman. Friday night cou1dn't have gotten there fast enough. He called her on Thursday night to confirm the date and to find out what movie she wanted to see, but he really just wanted to hear her voice (he was already in love and he didn't know it).

Now, there's up to a thirteen hour time difference from Southeast Asia and the East Coast, and his body clock hadn't adjusted yet. He found himself very sleepy at two in the afternoon and wide-awake at two in the morning. I tell you this because by the time he went to pick her up he was as sleepy as he could be. When he arrived at her house and she came downstairs he was immediately energized.

Love was an exceptionally beautiful woman. When he first met her at the bank, she was sitting behind the counter so he only saw her from the chest up. Now that he was seeing all of her he became a little self-conscience and he thought, "What is a good looking woman like this doing going out with me?" She had such an easy manner he immediately felt comfortable (maybe because of all the letters they had written to each other).

I must take a moment to express his differentiation between beautiful and good looking. Later in his life he built staging for fashion shows and he worked around many good looking women. Good looking can be described as being pleasing to the eye. Beautiful he defined as having a pleasing personality and being considerate of others. Exceptionally beautiful is a combination of beautiful and good looking. Love was an exceptionally beautiful woman.

At that time in her life he didn't think she really knew how attractive she was (she was nineteen and had just moved up from South Carolina). This was confirmed years later when they were talking about that first date and she made a comment that she didn't feel that she was pretty enough to go out with him. She said she thought he might be disappointed after he saw her in person. Boy, was she ever wrong. She had a beautiful face and a body that would stop traffic.

On leaving the house she said they had to stop by her sister's. He later found out he was being checked out. Apparently Love had a date with another Vietnam returnee and it hadn't been pleasant. On the way to the movie they talked and started to get to know each other. He didn't remember what movie they saw, but about halfway through it they were holding hands. And they were really comfortable with each other.

Now in those days, some men opened doors and removed their hats for ladies. They also always stood whenever a lady entered a room. These courtesies are lost in the new generation, but it was something you were taught to do for so long it became second nature. After the movie, they drove her back to her sisters and he helped her out of the car and walked her to the door. Back then a gentleman never expected a kiss on the first or second date, but Love thanked him for a nice evening and kissed him on the cheek. He asked her if he could call her, to which she said something he found most unusual She said, "You'd better." He was in love and on cloud nine, and it was the first of many wonderful experiences they had together...

I love you as,
the springtime grass is kissed by morning dew.
I love you as,
the deepest depth of oceans.
I love you as,
the highest peaks of mountain tops
I love you as,
the thunderous noise of waterfalls crashing sound
I love you as,
the heights of heaven, down to the deepest ground
I love you as,
just these mere words are failing to express
I love you as,
no entity, except for God himself
I love you as,
the ages past, and futures yet to come
I love you as,
my life is now, and will 'til it is long passed done
I love you as,
you're happy, I love you as you're sad
I love you for the good things, I love you as you're bad
I love you as,
the heights of passion, quenched fires of desire
I love you as,

eternal flames, are burning down in hell
I love you as,
though trying, these words could never tell
I love you as,
the flake of snow, would kiss the winter ground
I love you as,
the world will turn, and seasons turn around
I love you as,
much more today, than I did yesterday
I love you as,
these failing words, are trying to express
I love you as,
no entity, Except for God Himself
I love You as...

"Love made a decision that she wanted to be a flight attendant. Most of the time he was very supportive in anything she wanted to do if it made her happy. After a discussion about this, he saw that her mind was made up and there was nothing more he could do. After all, he did love her. To get the job, she had to take some tests and complete interviews. He drove her to the tests and interviews. When she was offered the job, she had to go to Flight Attendant College in Texas. She was gone for several weeks and during that time he was lost because they'd become almost inseparable. Their families must have thought they were joined at the hip for whenever you saw him you saw Love.

He just couldn't get enough of her, and he might have suffocated their relationship. Finally the day came when she was suppose to come home. However, she never made it because she and the other flight attendants had to spend the night at a hotel at Kennedy Airport until the next day when they got their assignments. That afternoon she called from

Kennedy Airport to say she wouldn't be able to leave until the following day because they were going to get their promotional assignments. She said they'd be at Kennedy Airport for about an hour before they left for the hotel. The time was about 5:15 PM, which meant it was the height of rush hour traffic in New York City which meant bumper to bumper traffic.

Without a second thought, he jumped in 'The 'Rooster' and became the wind. Nothing was going to stop him from seeing the woman he loved! Now this trip would normally take about an hour and a half at this time of day, but he made it with ten minutes to spare. I'm not going to tell you the kind of driving he had to do to get there in less than an hour, but he was sure there were people on the road who must have thought he was crazy for driving like that. You know, it's funny the crazy things a man will do for the love of a woman.

In the early summer of 1970, he was working as a sales representative selling greeting cards. The cards were developed by Malcolm X's Sister, and it was his job to sell them to the bookstores in the state colleges. Love was now working as a flight attendant, and since she didn't have any flights for a couple of days, he took her with him on one of his sales trips to four colleges. In the bookstore at the first school he asked for the manager. He made his best sales pitch about the quality and the price of the cards to the manager whose response could best be described as lukewarm. As you can guess, he got no sale.

After they got outside the store, Love started ribbing him about what a lousy salesman he was. He told her that if she thought she could do better he'd let her try the next sales call. When they got to the next bookstore, he just stood back and watched as she flashed her smile and charm on the Store manager. He never had a chance; when she finished making her pitch the man ordered forty-eight cartons. The same thing happened at the next two bookstores. By the time they got home that night he had more orders in that one day than he did the whole time he was on that job."

Growing Apart

After Love started working for the airline, her self confidence grew. She was becoming more aware of how physically attractive she was and discovering what affect this had on men. He knew all along the power she had on men because he used to see how they looked at her whenever they went out. She grew more attractive every day, and it was about this time that she started what he considered to be her favorite sport, flirting.

Love knew he was jealous, and took every chance she could to prove it. One night when her family was on vacation they had a party. There were quite a few people there, including several men he didn't know. They fried some chicken, made potato salad and bought a few bottles of wine. After the party began, Love started flirting, and quite naturally he got jealous. He decided since she wasn't going to be his date for the night he'd have a date with a half gallon of Bali Hai By the time everyone left around midnight he'd finished the bottle.

Before he knew it, he started to get sick. This gave new meaning to the phrase 'Sick for love.' He spent quite some time having an intimate relationship with the commode. After awhile he felt better, but he was still drunk and staggering into the walls. He told her that he was going home. She said that he was not going anywhere in his condition, and she took his car keys. He spent several hours crying in her arms asking her why she would do this to him. Somewhere in the wee hours of the morning, he fell asleep. A short while after this they got engaged.

In midst of raging winter blizzard I went to pick her up.
The road was just a sheet of ice in fact it flipped a truck.
Cars were skidding everywhere,
that none hit me, gave thanks.
The -Rooster- did three sixty, head first into a bank.
I couldn't see the damage, devoid of any light.
One thing that I was certain, we'd not get home tonight.
When I got to the parking lot and damage I could see.
Was then a deep depression, descended over me.
As soon as she could see me,
she knew there was something wrong.
I felt a whole lot better, in the safety of her arms.
She got a room and brought me in,
and I was real depressed.
She consoled with hugs and kisses,
and then she rubbed my neck.
In more romantic circumstances,
I'm sorry I can't say.
A man and woman made complete,
in a room at JFK..."

"Love had been working for the airline for some time and put in a request to be based out of LAX (Los Angeles California). During this time they had talked about getting married so they went shopping for an engagement ring. He personally believed that if he was really committed to Love, he shouldn't have to go to the expense of having to buy a ring just to show other people. Love insisted on the ring and, loving her the way he did, he gave in and bought the ring. He took her to Sakes Fifth Avenue in N.Y. and bought her a real cute powder blue mini dress for their engagement dinner.

The engagement dinner was one of the most wonderful events of his life. After all, he was going to marry the woman of his dreams. Shortly after this, Love's transfer came through. They'd talked about the transfer and decided she would spend the required time in LA and then transfer back. The day she left was the saddest day of his life. After all, he breathed that woman and when she left he was back to being that sick lonely puppy.

Now Love rarely got back in town since she didn't have much choice as to the routes she wanted to fly. The few times she did get back home, he was so happy. They'd go out together, but he noticed something had changed. She was getting more distant, and one night at dinner he caught her staring into space. The next day, he took her to the airport and kissed her good-bye as he had done so many times before...

Sometimes you just need a person,
To hear the things you say.
other times to be the object of pure loving lust.
More often times, and far, far better,
Is just a damned good friend... "

Jilted

"Love knew his work schedule and whenever she would fly into town and call him to pick her up. One day when he wasn't working, the phone rang and it was Love. As usual he was happy to hear from her. She said she was in Newark and needed to talk to him. He told her that he would come to the airport and pick her up. She said she wasn't at the airport, but that she was already at her brother's house. Fifteen minutes later he was ringing the bell.

When she answered the door, he tried to kiss her, which was his Custom. She turned her head and the kiss landed on her cheek. He figured she might have a cold and didn't want him to catch it, so he didn't think too much about it. Like I said, she was considerate. When they got upstairs, one of Love's flight attendant friends was sitting on the sofa, and she introduced them. When he looked back at Love she wouldn't look at him. This was something that had never happened before since she knew how much he loved her eyes. The tension in the room was suddenly so thick you could cut it with a knife. Then after a long moment of silence, Love said she couldn't marry him and handed him the engagement ring wrapped up in a tissue.

What happened next could only have been described as a perfect paradox. Love and her friend were suddenly as giddy as schoolgirls as he stood there in silence staring at the ring. Then they started chatting about some guy named Jim. He felt like he was suffocating and the next thing he knew he was in his car and he didn't know if he'd said, "Good-bye." It would be eight long years before he saw Love again and it would be hard and painful road back...

In my life, I've done some things for which I'm happy

I've done some things of which I'm proud

I've done few things for which I'm sorry

But the sorriest is, letting you get away

Unrequited love is such sweet sadness..."

Chapter 6

The Long Road Back

Uncle Question was about to continue the story when Grandma called Grandpa from inside the house, "Wisdom, would you please come here and take this garbage out." Grandpa yelled back, "Cummin Puddin," He excused himself and went to the door saying, "You've gotta learn how to keep peace out of confusion, when women folk ask you to do things, I always find it's easier to comply and avoid the hassles." Then he went into the house, while the three of us sat in the quiet of the early evening. A couple of minutes Grandpa returned to the porch and his rocking chair, and Uncle Question continued the story.

"For this young man it was a long road back. And the first thing he had to do was to get Love out of his system. He was in a fog the first month or so after she left. He couldn't eat or sleep, and kept asking himself why she'd do this to him. He lost weight and his family was starting to worry about him. He really only had one good friend he could talk to and he was away at college, so he internalized his feelings. He was so depressed at one point he even considered suicide. He didn't have a gun, and after all the blood he'd seen in the war, cutting his wrist was out of the question.

Somehow he got past this point without harming himself. And he silently carried his grief until the pain, sorrow and self-pity forced him to tears. One day he started crying, and couldn't stop for almost two days. Afterwards, he had to admit he felt a little better. Love had engrained herself in his soul and he couldn't get her out. His only regrets were those that related to Love's family. He had developed relationships with some of them and erroneously assumed because she didn't want him, they didn't want him. He also knew being around them would bring back painful memories.

Later that year he got a new job with another company and they sent him to school. This kept him busy and he didn't have as much time to think about her. But in the back of his mind, she was always there and he'd catch himself in daydreams thinking about her. He hadn't had a date since she left and he really didn't want one. His best friend was home from school for the holidays, and decided to have a New Years party. His friend told him he had to bring a date to the party, so he started looking for someone to ask. One day while shopping, he started talking to a cashier. He asked if she had a date for New Year's Eve, and when she said she didn't, he asked if she'd like to attend the party, and she agreed.

That first date turned out to be a lot of fun, and they went out again. However, he kept thinking that there was something strange about their relationship and he couldn't figure it out. After about a month of dating, she broke up with him. As politely as she could, she told him that she had found someone else. There was a rage building in him regarding women. This rage festered to the point where he perceived women were the cause of his pain and he was going to make all women pay by declaring war on them

He decided he would go after women with a vengeance and break their hearts just like his had been broken. He didn't trust woman and subconsciously he hated them. He developed weapons and tactics to fight this war. His weapons were manners, patience and the powers of observation. I've already told you about manners, so we'll move on to patience. Given enough time to study something, you can overcome it. A woman is no different and you need only to take the time to find out what piques their curiosity and go for their heart. He knew that if you took the time to find their curiosity, you can have them.

He'd learned from The Committee, (a group of women friends), if you really want to know about a woman don't watch her, but watch other women watch her. Women give off signals in the company of other women and if you read these signals you've got it made. Many women are socialized to view other women as competition and they act that way. We now move on to the targets.

The targets in this war were good-looking women. All others need not apply. The closer the resemblance they were to Love, the better. Now you must also remember this was during the sexual revolution and there were quite a few women into one-night stands. These easy women were discarded as targets. The objective here was a broken heart-theirs. Looking back, he wouldn't condone what he did, but he was in pain and someone had to pay for the cause. He made up rules to fight his war and to him this was okay.

Human are creatures of habit, and in this regard he was no different than anyone else. He started to go to the clubs, and over a six-month period, he was going to the same clubs on the same nights. One night he was sitting at the bar of a club talking to the bartender. Anyone who's spent time in a New York bar in the winter knows that when the door opens a draft comes in. When he felt the draft on his back, he glanced over his shoulder to see who it was. He spotted a very tall, and I mean tall (six foot), version of Love.

She was absolutely gorgeous, and except for the height and the fact she had light brown eyes, she bore a very close resemblance to Love. When she saw him she smiled and came over and asked if anyone was sitting on the stool next to him. He told her no, and invited her to take the seat. (He was thinking she'd make a perfect target in his war). When she gave him his favorite opening line, 'Hello, I'm Tina. How are you doing this evening?' Smiling at him, she added, 'Have you heard that line before?' He was floored! She explained she was a graduate student at NYU and was doing research, and men like him were the subject.

She told him she had been watching him for months in the various clubs and noticed he always talked to the same kind of women, in her words, 'Kinda like me.' Again, he was floored. For the next hour or so she exposed his game to him. She then asked if the person he was trying to get back at knew about it, and he said, 'No.' Then she said, 'You respect women but you really don't like them,' he knew he was not winning his war on women. By now he was feeling really guilty and was getting up to go when she said, 'You're one of the smoothest I've seen, and you have a baby face. You've got a good heart, next time, try it for real'

He never saw Tina again. but he could still hear those words, 'You respect women but you really don't like them.' When he got outside he said out loud, 'Love, I still love you.' That was when he finally started to heal

During his war on women, he had gotten back together with the woman he took to the New Years party. For some strange reason, he began to think that this woman might be having some gender preference conflicts. He first noticed it in the way she dressed. From time to time she became distant and cold, but he tried to hang in there. In his mind a little voice kept saying, 'There has to be something better. '

During the periods when her preferences changed for women he would hang in as long as he could. He could never understand what it was that kept him in this on-again off-again relationship. But he would reach an emotional limit, and then he would be forced to leave. He still thought of Love and her memory continued to plague his potential relationships. Some of the women he dated told him he was too picky, but it wasn't in his nature to just settle. He needed more than that and had seen more than a few relationships fail because one of the partners was willing to settle, only to find out later it wouldn't work. Love had set a standard and any new relationship had to measure up.

One day, after eight years of this, Love called him from her brother's house and said she wanted to see him. After the initial shock, he ran to see her. When he saw her he knew that he loved her more now than ever before. It was different now - not the passion it had been - but it had a comfortable feel of maturity. He'd been so passionately in love with her before, he never learned to read her. But he got the impression that she wanted to tell him something, which she never did. When he left, he had a warm and fuzzy feeling and it would be four more years before he saw her again...

Love is pain and sorrow, torment, sacrifice, hurt and anger.
Love is trust and doubt, jealousy, and many sleepless nights.
Love is Beautiful, and unrequited love is such sweet sadness...

Sitting on the porch, we lapsed into one of those silent moments, when from inside the house Aunt Ester called out "Question would you please go to the car and bring me in that shopping bag in the trunk." "Yes Dear," he answered and without hesitation got up. He excused himself and started down the steps of the porch. On his way down the steps he said, "You know a lot of men complain about all the things their women ask them to do. What they always seem to forget is all the things they do for you. I mean think about it, any woman that washes your funky draws must love you, and I don't like to argue."

I thought about this for a moment when it occurred to me that I had never heard my grandparents or my Mom and Dad for that matter have an argument. I said to Grandpa. "Grandpa have you ever had an argument with Grandma?" He said, "Junior all couples have disagreements. Its how you resolve those disagreements that count." I realized that he hadn't answered my question so I asked him? "'But when was the last time you had an argument with Grandma?" "That would have been in the fall of 1978." When he said 1978, Dad and I started laughing and wondering how he remembered the year. Grandpa continued, "Don't laugh," he said, I remember it because of what happened that year. At breakfast she said she thought I should start harvesting the crop on the south-end. I told her I was going to start in two weeks. She insisted I should start right away.

We went back and forth a couple of times and finally she didn't say anymore about it. As for me, I figured I was going to start when I was good and ready. I was thinking to myself: I'm not going to let that woman tell me when to harvest. About four days later it started to rain, and it rained night and day for almost a week. Needless to say, I lost almost half that crop. Now that was bad enough, but then I had to apologize to Essence, and that was the really hard part. After that I vowed I'd pay more attention when she spoke of those matters because she rarely did and when she did she was usually right. You know, too often we men let our egos and our stubbornness get in the way of the common sense advice we get nom those who care give us. What I learned from that experience was those who care about us never lead us astray. If they say something important we should listen. "

When Uncle Question returned from his errand, he asked what he had missed. Dad filled him in on the question I asked Grandpa, and what Grandpa's answer had been. He laughed and said "As I see it, most disagreements are generally started over little things. Then the parties get so entrenched on a position from which they refuse to bend, which blows the whole thing up into a big issue. Then Dad said, "Many couples I've known have fought most often over two things, the intervention of relatives or friends and money.

As far as relatives are concerned, you'd be well advised to keep them out of your marital affairs. You may choose to talk with them about it, but it will ultimately come down to being able to talk to your partner. So it's important to always keep the communication open. As for money, your Mom and I have never fought over money because we agreed to the hundred dollar rule early in our relationship." I asked him, "What's the hundred dollar rule?" He said, "Any single purchase of a hundred or more, must be discussed first. You see I'm not likely to win an argument with your mom and I learned early on...

With the woman you love, you can't win an argument, so don't you even try, because it makes no sense.
Takes too much effort, and you're soon gonna find, she's gonna be right about 95 percent of the time. Then you gotta back track, and swallow your pride.
And go through the pain of having to apologize.
So the sooner you learn, and come to your sense, With the woman you love, you can't win an argument..."

"It's Unfortunate that women have caused a good man to go to these extreme measures, but until you confront that first love you cannot begin to heal. You respect women, but you don't like them very much."

Chapter 7

Guy Talk

We were in one of those reflective moments, as the sun started its inevitable downward movement to night. A breeze had come up and the crickets started their evening song. We were suddenly snapped out of the moment by the smell of perfume and a sound out on the sidewalk.

Wooof!

All the heads on the porch turned in the direction of the sound. As the breeze picked up, the scent of perfume was heavy. Coming down the sidewalk was Ms. Precious Jones, the daughter of Mrs. Lulea Jones. She was heavily made up and as she passed we all spoke to her, but she continued on as if we didn't exist. Grandpa said, "We have to forgive that child, for she had some problems with men and right now she's mad with all men." After a moment of thought, Grandpa said, 'That child sure wears a lot of perfume...

Now did you ever notice,
How women wear perfume?
Faint whiff will always make you search,
what course they might be on.
While others smell before they're here,
and long after they're gone..."

Dad then commented, "She sure wears a lot of makeup too, and then he broke into...

Don't take these lines literally, for its not meant to be.
But rather as a warning, to save some feelings deep.
Some women put on makeup, it's like an armored shield.
And once it's on, it covers, what should really be revealed.
If you want to know them, must catch them when it's off.
And you ever love them, til you've seen them in the rough.
Some wear it well and you don't notice,
put on for perfect light, but when it is wrong,
other women snicker, and talk about that sight .
Be careful of that makeup, be cautious what you see.
It might be hiding more, than what they want revealed... "

We all laughed and then Grandpa said, "You know, women have a difficult time out here today. With all the pressure to look just right, act just right and think like a millennium woman, they're almost as confused as men about what their roles are. In my day it was much easier. Men for the most part did the chasing except of course, on Sadie Hawkins day." We all started laughing again. He then he said, "That was the one day women could chase you. But there were also clear rules of behavior. If you really wanted to deal with the decent women you followed the rules. Rules are so muddled, I'd be damned if it don't seem like there are no rules. "

"People gotta have rules, even if it's personal rules, cause you gotta look at yourself in the mirror. If you don't like what you see, the world won't either. The problem seems to be there are too many choices. Sometimes they make no choice because there are too many options. This causes them stress which could have been avoided if they'd made a selection. Every mistake is a chance to learn something. So I don't see why folks don't go with their gut, make a pick and be prepared to learn something and totally avoid the stress. Now you take dating, in my day it was called courtin.

You knew that you were gonna pick her up at her house, go in and meet her folks. Not just on the first date but every date. Now-a-days women gotta meet men in well lit, crowded places to know if it's safe to go someplace else with him. Another thing, in my day you always knew that you were gonna pay. Now-a-days folks don't know who's gonna pay. Women's liberation didn't help either, except to confuse men even further, and we were already confused. You take down at the barber shop the other day. These young fellas were talking about being invited on dates then getting stuck with the check. It got me to thinking...

She's long since burned her bra, and changed her name to Ms.
Doors once opened by someone else, she opens for herself.
In total liberation she goes through every day.
That's total liberation until it's time to pay.
Should she grant you opportunity, and both of you go out.
Her position on this subject leaves you in some doubt.
It turns to a convenience, which really blows your mind.
For it seems she's only liberated, until the check arrives.
A most convenient position, until it comes to cash.
It's in this situation, her conviction seems to lack.
She's the ultimate of feminist, as it would suit her whim.
But when it comes to money, she's strict old fashion then.
I believe in liberation, it was so before my time.
I say draft them in the army, and equal pay for equal time.
But I don't like wishy washy, in other words hypocrites.
To stand on a position, as it would suit the wish.
For you must be ere consistent, to gain credibility,
stand strong on your conviction, what ever comes to be.
Not convenience or a defense, to cull what's undesired.
As in she's very liberated, until the check arrives ...

Another thing that makes it harder on men and women is all the sex conjured images of perfection in media. When you add to this all the high tech stuff like computers, cell phones and faxes designed to help communication, nobody really communicates. We've gotten so focused on the instruments we forgot they're just tools to help do better what we didn't do very well in the first place. Since people don't have time for conversations, they never really get to know anyone. Then they can't understand why they don't have meaningful relationships.

"A good relationship takes the same thing now it always has, patience. With all the push button conveniences now, some folks are erroneously lulled into believing they can push a button and instantly have a good relationship. The one constant in building anything of worth is time. It takes time to cultivate, and time to understand the problems that prevent cultivation. Developing a good relationship is the same as growing crops. It won't happen instantly and it requires a lot of work and a little luck."

At that moment my mind went back to the young woman who'd passed, for the scent of her perfume was still in the air. So I asked Grandpa what he meant about Precious Jones having man problems. Grandpa said, "You remember I said that people are caught up in the media hype about perfection?" I remember," I said. 'Well, Miss Precious Jones is a victim of that hype. In her case it has to do with weight. She used to be right portly, if you get my meaning. Then she lost a bunch of weight and with it she gained a whole new set of problems." After a pause he started...

She used to weigh one eighty, Was sure of who were friends.
Now that she's lost that fifty, The phone it always rings.
And now this new dilemma, She never had before.
Does he want her for her body, or does he want much more?
She now must learn new lessons, which leaves her in a fog.
Too many bad experiences, she now thinks all men are dogs.
For what was once so simple, is now the other Way.
A weighty new dilemma, For fifty pounds of weight...

Like I said, women have as many problems out here today as the men and a few more. They've got to get their hair done and their nails and such. And then there's this thing about their clothes. Every season of the year they gotta get somethin' new that's awfully expensive. Now think about skirts for a minute. In my day, no way a woman was gonna show her thighs. If you got a glimpse of some ankle you were seeing a lot. Any woman who wore a skirt higher than mid calf was considered I believe you call em hoochies. Today, women wear their skirts half way to their necks and it's okay. That reminds me of the Oprah show the other day.

She had a woman guest who came out in a mini skirt. She sat down crossed her legs and commenced tryin to pull the skirt down. Now this didn't make any sense to me because there was nothing to pull down in the first place. During the whole interview she was constantly pullin on that skirt. And it was a major distraction watching her do it. Now it seems to me that if you're gonna be on national TV you'd wear something that you don't need to be pulling on every two seconds.

In my day women had a mystique about them. This mystery helped when they were dating because it raised a curiosity. The first servant of discovery is curiosity. Most women now don't have any mystery about them. They show all and that takes the fun out of dating. It seems they're advertising a product that's not worth buying. "Junior did you ever notice that you take second looks at women wearing long dresses?" I thought about this for a second, and realized he was right, and I said, "I never really thought about it, but you're right, I do." Then Grandpa said, "That's because of the mystery." Cousin Doris says each generation loses more values and we've gotten to the point where everything is out there for everyone to see. Just look at the movies and listen to the lyrics today, not to mention all the booty shakin videos.

In my day, when you saw a movie and they got to the part for the love scene the screen went black and it was left to your imagination. Now-a-days they show you everything. If you listen to Rap songs by the young folks today they're always singing about soapin' up and sexin' down. Nothing's left to the imagination, and imagination is the first servant of curiosity. I think this has desensitized us to what appropriate behavior is. That's why there is so much rape goin' on now.

You know, it seems to me that it's a pretty sorry man that has to resort to rippin' off some lovin' from an unwilling partner. When you think about it, it doesn't seem like it would be much fun anyway. Things now are worse sexually than they were during the sexual revolution. Men in particular seem to have forgotten the meaning of the word no. Many men seem to think if they spend a little money on a woman they are entitled to some lovin' in return. If they took a little more time they might find out they didn't want make love to that woman anyway.

We drifted into in one of those quiet reflective periods, and Dad broke the reflection when he said, "Things now have changed around so much everyone's become skeptical about almost everybody from the politicians to preachers. People we once respected seem to be running a game on us. It's the same thing in this new sexual revolution. In my day there were more virgins trying to act like they weren't. Today there are more non-virgins trying to act like they are. A lotta folks just don't take the time to develop friendships.

The key to all long-term relationships is friendship. A friend is the most important thing you can make in this world. With a true friend you can be alone, but you're not alone. You can argue with a friend and still know their gonna be your friend. Seems young folk don't know how to make a true friend these days. The funny thing is they use the word all the time and have little understanding as to what it means. Folks dating today will introduce someone as their friend. Two months later they're introducing someone else as their friend and it's obvious they're dating. Many people forget that the great equalizer in all things is time. If .you try to rush time you only wind up rushing yourse1f.

Young people now get so caught up in peer pressure and following the herd they lose themselves. The current herd instinct is obtaining material things and they mistakenly think these things will make them happy. Yet they soon find out after getting them they're not happy. This is because they don't have any true friends and aren't willing to investment in the time it takes to develop them. People want a guarantee for everything and the only guarantee in life is that there will be change. A good friend is sure nice to have through all that...

There is no time anymore for just plain talk,
to get a different viewpoints, no time to take a walk.

They toil in desperation, acquiring wealth to buy a Benz.
And for this we've lost ability, to acquire trusted friends.

So thus we face the bad times, sulking alone at home.
In same situation with a friend, you'd never be alone.

Seems everybody's out for, whatever they can gain.
It didn't use to be this way, but now it's such a shame.

Its politics and lawyers, with everything at stake.
The contracts are now volumes, to cover any harm.

It used to be so simple, when hand and word were bond.
As lawyers have now changed it, those days forever gone.

It things that are important, caught up in following trends.
It's better a Mercedes, than long time trusted friend...

When Dad finished, Uncle Question said, "That friendship thing reminds me of how our young man learned about friendship with women. These women, who we'll call The Committee, helped him on the long road back from depths of his broken heart. "

Chapter 8

The Committee

Uncle Question continued with the story. "Before I get back to the story, I'd like to make a few qualifying statements. First, any man that doesn't have the discipline to control his debt or his penis will always be a slave in some form. You minored in economics so I don't have to tell you about debt. But giving in to the urges of the penis can for obvious reason cause a lifetime of aggravation and debt. The sooner you can control thinking with the little head, the sooner you can get to more important parts of your life.

I'd suggest to every young man get himself some good platonic women friends. These women can dispel many of the false myths we men tend to have about women. They can also serve as an evaluation board for any woman that you might consider having a serious relationship with. Remember when you're dating you are dealing with your sexual urges. These urges often blind you to some of the realities you might not be able to cope with later when the passion dies down.

There's no more comfortable feeling for a man than to be able to sit among a group of women and have them feel comfortable with you. There's no pressure to make a good impression, or any impression for that matter. It's nice to just be able to be yourself What's even better is when they feel comfortable enough with you to maybe let you into the realm known as girl talk. Its here you'll learn to most about women which you can use in your own dating experience. All you have to do is sit quietly and listen. Men and women can be best of friends as long as they keep the relationship out of the bed. This is because women of good traditional moral character often can't separate their hearts from their bodies. Now the young man in our story had some women friends he considered to be sisters and they taught him well. They taught him, no matter what a woman says, and she will mean it when she says it, if she likes you and thinks enough of you to give you her body, her heart will go with it.

His relationship with The Committee was such that he could talk to them about anything and he could get a woman's perspective on various issues. It was also these women who helped him understand that some of the myths he had developed about women weren't correct. It got to the point where he trusted their opinion so much that any woman he was dating he'd introduce to The Committee. They never guided him wrong, because while he was thinking with his glands they'd be reading the woman.

It was also these women that helped him change his mind about hating women. They did this by allowing him to see that not all women were the deceitful, conniving beasts he thought they were. He also learned any woman he dated who had a problem with his women friends was also the kind of women who thought you were not supposed to do one of the most natural things God put on this earth, and that is look at a woman. Looking is okay; in fact it's natural. If you're dating a woman that has a problem with this, I would suggest you dump her because she has no confidence in herself

It sure didn't hurt our young man's ego whenever he went out with The Committee. Guys would be trying to figure out what was up because he had all these beautiful women with him. And, they thought it even more unusual that these women all got along. Man, were those men dumb. It was so simple, they had a great friendship. If the women ran into a persistent guy or didn't want to be bothered, he became an instant boyfriend. This also worked in reverse. To these women the young man's life was an open book. And at times he felt that they knew him better than he knew himself.

When he discovered his wife (one of The Committee), he never stood a chance because the rest of them all ganged up on him in her behalf. To this day he blames them for him being married, but he had to admit it was the best thing that happened to him You see, The Committee was looking out for his welfare and he didn't even know it. Again you can see how important that friendship thing is. You're probably wondering how the young man in our story met The Committee. The fact of the matter is he met The Committee's Chairwoman first."

Chapter 9

Meeting the Chairwomen

Before Uncle Question could continue we were again distracted by a sound out on the sidewalk.

Wooof !

All heads on the porch turned in the direction of the sound. It was a woman I didn't remember seeing before. Even though she was about forty or so, she had an incredible body. When she was still a good way off: Grandpa said sorta to himself: "Leslie Gideon." Then he said to us, "Her name's Leslie Gideon and she's been the subject of more barber shop conversations than a Super Bowl" In his best deacon voice he said, "'It's been said her moral fabric might be a little bit torn. Seems she has a bit of a reputation, if you know what I mean. Some folks call her, Let's-Get-It-On. Grandma Essence says she's a Hoochie Mama, whatever that means."

When Ms Gideon saw us on the porch, there was a noticeable change in her walk. Not so much in the pace, but more in the sway of her hips. It seemed she wanted to make sure we saw her. Reaching the gate she stopped, and placing a hand on her hip, with a smile and husky voice said, "Howdy boys, how ya'll doin this evening?" Grandpa answered and the rest of us nodded. "How do, Miss Gideon, how you feelin?" "'I'm doin marvelously well thank you." she said. 'That's right nice to hear", Grandpa said. Then he asked, "Have you met my family?" "I don't believe I've had the honor," she said as she headed up the walk to the porch. When she got to the top step she paused as Grandpa began making introductions.

Ms Gideon's reaction was the same for Dad as it was for Uncle Question. With her hand extended, she stepped directly in front of each and with a smile she, "It's nice to meet you" Her eyes went from their groin to the ring finger and then to their the eyes. When she got to me and eyes finally met mine her smile had broadened as she held onto my hand a little too long. Then she said, "'It's really nice, to meet you. As I spoke to her I felt very uncomfortable because her eyes were focused on my groin. When she let go of my hand, we all started talking. about the weather and stuff.

After the conversation wavered and Ms Gideon said she had to be movin' on. She shook everybody's hand again, looked them in the face and said how nice it was to meet them. Again when she got to me, her eyes were focused on my groin, and again that uncomfortable feeling came over me. It was as if l was naked in front of her. As she went out the walk, she said over her shoulder, "'It was nice meetin you all" She continued out the walk, and looked over her shoulder at me and said, "'If you're not doing anything later meet me at Jake's Place and I'll buy you a drink." I said. 'Thank you very much, and it was nice meeting you."

When her back was completely turned I allowed my gaze to wander down from her shoulders to her rear end. And what a rear end it was, as I watched each move of her exaggerated walk. I didn't realize I was staring until suddenly I had this feeling that someone was staring at me. When I looked to my right, everyone was staring at me and smiling. Uncle Question said, 'The more you drink the better they look.' And she looks good before you drink the first drop." We all laughed. Then Grandpa said, "Don't let that exterior fool you, that girl's a Harvard graduate and one of the finest CPA's anywhere. She just has a few problems. Her parents were real strict and they're also two of the coldest people I've ever met. When she got accepted at Harvard they insisted she attend. She wanted to go to State. She was okay when she left, but when she returned after four years she wasn't quite the same. I think her emotionless parents are the cause of her problems. She sleeps around because she's still looking for the hugs, he never gave her."

Uncle Question continued with the story saying, "I was talking about The Committee and how the young man in the story met them. As every group has a leader, it shouldn't be surprising that he met the Chairwoman first. They met at a college homecoming weekend. She had taken a bus down to meet her girlfriend at school He had driven to spend the weekend with his best friend who attended the same school. Sometime during the weekend, they all hooked up. He found out she lived in the town next to his. When found out she'd taken a bus to get there, he offered her a ride home suggesting she could cash in the other half of the bus ticket. She accepted his offer and they rode home together.

Now you have to remember this was shortly after Love had left him and he was still in the depths of his sorrow. But unless there's something wrong with you, you can't spend eight hours in a car with someone and not get know them at least a little bit. She was a tall, young attractive woman who was easy to talk to. He spent a good deal of time talking about Love and she patiently listened with a sympathetic ear."

At this point, Uncle Question broke from the story and said, "'That reminds me of something I heard a psychologist say on a radio show. They were talking about relationships and she said many women forget you can start a good relationship with a man by simply lending a sympathetic ear.

They were talking about what men were seeking in their women, when she quoted...

'A beautiful woman intrigues him, An intelligent woman stimulates him, But the sympathetic woman gets him.'

'Well that's how our young man met The Committee Chairwoman and it was through her that he met the rest of the Committee. They were all relatives and friends of hers and they spent a lot of time in her kitchen discussing many subjects over the years.

Chapter 10

The Kitchen

Uncle Question continued the story saying, "Mama says to get to know people, you gotta sit in their kitchen.. The parlor's for show, but the kitchen's to know. She also says, 'A man should never marry a woman that won't talk with him in her kitchen. If a woman won't take you into her kitchen, its probably because of two things. The first being, she doesn't know where it is. Or second, if she does know where it is, she might not know what to do in it.' In any case, a woman that can't cook has taken a major piece of artillery out of her arsenal of how to get a man. In the history of the world, billions of men have lost their hearts though their stomachs. After all, eating is one of the two sensual pleasures.

Our young man owes a great deal to the women in that kitchen. He was really down in the dumps about losing Love. It was only fitting that the War On Women truly ended in that kitchen. Twelve years of warfare and lost battles, waged with wounds to the heart that were always treated in that kitchen. Twelve years of sharing each other's dates, affairs, marriages, divorces, hopes and dreams. But the treatment was always the same; good food, bad wine and the best medicine of all, laughter. All the time they were developing the deepest of bonds. They taught each other many things, and more importantly they learned about themselves.

They taught him how to watch women watching women and how to pick out prospects. He also learned about pick-up lines and how to separate a woman from a herd. They learned from him how to go out in a group and still make themselves available to any interested, but shy guy, who might want to approach one of them. As you can see, they had an unusual relationship. One of the many important things he learned was how to relax around women and to be himself And, he learned about sex and how to do it right from just listening to what they said.

Now-a-days folks take themselves too seriously. Men and women can't do one of the most natural things anymore, and that is flirt. If either party makes a gesture or comment it's' grounds for a law-suit. Women like to feel they are alluring and, as he saw it, flirting with these women was safe. If one of them had on something he liked he was allowed to say so. And they were all beautiful women.

Now I want you to think how funny this sight must have been. This tall dorky guy with a baby face and glasses he was always pushing up on his nose. And here he was hanging out with these beautiful women. They were all fine and had no problem getting men. In fact, he met many of their men friends. The only problem was they always seemed to attract the wrong kind of men.

As a man with normal urges, even he had fantasies about one member in particular. She made the best spiced potato salad this side of New Orleans. Spicy, that would be the way to describe her. She was a tall Scorpio with light brown eyes and a body to die for, and she knew it. She also knew he had the hots for her. From time to time she would tease him by putting on a pair of short shorts and one of her father's shirts tied in a knot at the front so that her midriff was exposed. Man was she somethin."

Teasing

"Because the young man was taught to stand up when a lady entered a room, he was always exposed to playful bump of her hip and on occasion, a frontal grind when she'd walk by him. As you might have expected, that really turned him on which would make him fantasize about her. Because she knew him, there was no way he was going to sneak up on her. Besides, she had helped teach him everything he knew about women. He'd say playfully to her, "I had this dream about you. We were doing the nasty, and I was tearin' your body up." Then she'd give him a sultry smile and say something like, "Don't even try it, I'd break you in half" Then everybody laughed. But the young man's mind would inevitably drift to the fantasy. And if he could have figured out a way to jump her bones, he would have.

We've already mentioned that our young man was late in developing, and this included his physical development as well But years of construction work and working with his upper body, he had filled out. He had one of those wash board stomachs that everybody now goes to the gym to get, and a twenty-nine inch waist and big thighs. All in all he was turning into a strapping young piece of manhood. And, he took his occasional shot at teasing the members of The Committee.

He'd put on a pair of cut-off jeans rolled up to about mid thigh. Then he'd put on a tee shirt cut off at mid chest. He'd buy a half gallon of wine and go sit in that kitchen with The Committee. After a few drinks they'd start to sneak secret looks at his body and later they actually start to stare at him. Inevitably, one of the committee would make a suggestive comment and they'd all laugh. The ice would be broken and nothing would come of it because they were all good friends. That was their bond, and nobody was going to do anything to mess it up. They were all going through the same kinds of relationship problems. Because they could talk about anything, as you might guess the subject of traps and games often came up."

From inside the house Mom called out to Dad:

"Reason would you please come here and give me a hand." As Dad got up from his seat he said, "I love to feel needed. One of the primary needs that people have, is the need to feel needed. "Then he went into the house, and a minute later Mom and Dad stepped out on the porch with a pitcher of lemonade and four glasses. She handed a glass to Grandpa and Uncle Question, then smiling at me she went back into the house. Dad handed me a glass and took his seat. We all took a sip, then Uncle Question continued the story saying, "Where was I? Oh yeah, I was talking about traps and games."

Chapter 11

Traps and Games

On the string

"He met Bobbi at a party. She seemed nice enough, and they had an interesting conversation. By the end of the evening they exchanged phone numbers. He called her a couple of days later and they started going out. This continued for a few months and during their dates. he was always the perfect gentleman. One night after a date they got back to his place very late, she always met him at his place for all the dates. During this time, the young man had never tried to put a move on this lady. But on this night he invited her to spend the night because it would have taken her almost an hour to drive back home. She agreed and they went to bed together. Since he wasn't in a habit of looking in women's purses, it never occurred to him that women usually did not carry nightgowns with them.

After getting in bed, they continued the conversation. Being a man, he had to make a move and that cut the conversation short. After all, they had been going out for some time. He had more than a few fantasies about her, and he'd spent quite a bit of money on her, too. Now all that time and money were going to be repaid. They were laying back to back, so he rolled over and put an arm over her to hold her.

She gently took his hand put it back on his side of the bed and said. 'There'll be none of that. We're going to be .Friends, and friends don't screw each other." After a couple of minutes the young man thought he'd give the lady a second chance to say no. (They say, 'you should always give a lady two chances to say no.) He put his arm over her again. This time she removed his hand a little more forcefully, and said 'I said there would be none of that.' The young man got the message and accepted the fact that they'd just be Friends. That was the first of many times they slept together as friends."

Then Uncle Question departed from the story by saying, 'Wow you'll have to excuse me if I interrupt the story for a moment, but I feel a need to point out something about language. Americans don't speak English. They speak many dialects of English. Now-a-days we've got this new element thrown in to confuse us even more. And it seems like folks are now trying not to offend anyone anymore in their speech. It's called political correctness. By doing this, people can desensitize folks from really bad situations, and at the same time, keep themselves from feeling guilty." Then Dad said, "It's called Psycho-Linguistics and it's really a way for people to avoid bad situations rather than change them. The problems continue to get worse because they changed the language so problems don't sound so bad."

After a moment of reflection, Uncle Question said, "We speak many dialects of English. Quite often we use words and phrases to mean the complete opposite of the word or phrase. For example; bad, in certain American dialects, can actually mean good. Now let's try a phrase, say, sleeping together. Two words that mean someone is sleeping with someone else which may or may not infer having sex. That brings us back to our story.

This couple was sleeping together in the literal sense. To this young man it had become normal because in his lifetime he'd slept with far more women than he ever had sex with.

She slept on the couch and he slept on the chair, or vice versa. But that was okay because he could honestly say he was sleeping with a woman. With people being the way they were, their minds would infer that he was having sex. And since a gentleman doesn't kiss and tell he could avoid getting razzed by the fellas for not getting any. He only had to state a literal truth to get over, no implication required.

This leads us back to our young man and that lady he was sleeping with. Their relationship continued like it had for some time, but they didn't see each other that often. When they did, she would call him and suggest they get together. They'd go out and she'd tease him just enough with a special outfit or her movements on the dance floor to keep him interested. And, of course they'd end up in bed sleeping. And this gets to the irony of this relationship.

Now contrary to what some women might think, the dating situation is tough on a man, especially if he is a good man. Men go through dating dry spells just like women do, and he was going through one of those spells. The unusual thing was when these two went out, she was like a magnet for some of the finest women he ever saw making advances to him. Being a gentleman, he was obliged to turn them down, which brings us back to The Committee."

Bonding

"Our young man's relationship with the Committee had gone on for five years. Five years of communicating with beautiful intelligent women. Five years of problems and solutions and learning about each other, and more importantly learning about themselves. He watched and listened while developing solid friendships. They had long reached a level of comfort with no pretenses. One day while sitting in that kitchen he mentioned he was dating. They all turned to look at him at once. Almost in unison they said, 'The monk is dating?' He had managed to hide his secret from them for some time, but one word had their attention and that word was dating. Up until this time he had used the word seeing. He'd never brought any of his dates to meet the Committee. And now one word had blown his game.

They started pumping him for details. The first question was, 'How long have you known her, and how did you meet her?' Questions were coming at him so fast and from so many different directions it seemed they were all being asked at once. Before he knew it, they were extracting information faster than water through a sieve. The final question was 'Is she any good in bed'? He responded with, 'A gentleman doesn't tell.' This didn't deter them from getting this last piece of information. He resorted to the one phase that always worked with the guys, "We're sleeping together." There was only one problem; these weren't guys and the ploy didn't work. With more pressure, he finally gave them what many women want, details. "Almost as soon as he had finished giving them the last detail they all looked at each other and almost in unison said, 'Trap' He said, 'Trap, what trap. What do you mean?' Any person that ever spent any time in the bush during the Vietnam War takes the word trap seriously.

This was the first time he'd ever talked at length about any of his dates. They were all looking at each other and a couple of them were smiling. Then the Chairwoman spoke. saying, 'Let's look at the facts. The woman is twenty eight, she just happens to carry a night gown in her pocketbook, which most women don't do. You don't see her that often, and she always meets you at your place. She just happens to sleep with you but she won't let you touch her. Have I got this right?' "Yes" he said as he began to realize that these women looked at his situation from a totally different perspective. Then the Chair-woman said, 'Mister what we have here is a classic String Job. This woman has another man, she's probably not sure where the relationship is going to go, but just in case things don't work out, you're the fall back guy.'

"Our man wasn't sure what to make of all this, especially in light of this new perspective. So he did what any gentleman would do and defended the woman's honor though it was a weak effort. Then the Chairwoman said, 'This woman is going to make an attempt to have sex with you, mark my word.' The young man hadn't heard from the lady for some time', but she called two weeks later and they got together.

After their date, they ended up in his bed as usual; but this time was different. There was a tension that hadn't been there before. He picked up on it and asked the lady, 'Is there something wrong? You've been strangely silent all evening.' Without a word she rolled over on top of him and kissed him. He responded by saying, 'You said we were just going to be friends, and there'd be none of that. As he was pushing her off, his mind was focusing on the words of the Chairwoman. 'This woman is going to make an attempt to have sex with you.' Well there was no sex that night and the lady went to sleep. He couldn't sleep since his mind kept racing. He still couldn't grasp the realization that The Committee had predicted the situation so correctly. It was at this moment he decided to use the Committee as an evaluation and clearing board for his future dates. Oh yes, and one other very important thing came out of this situation.

The next day our man went to see the Chair-woman. When he told her about the experience she didn't say anything, she just smiled and they went on to another conversation. But this took the relationship with The Committee to a different better level It was after this that the young man was let into that secret realm that few men get to go. This is the realm of Girl Talk.

Girl talk is where a man can learn what women really think about. Not in the usual superficial way, but rather in an emotional way. But you can't get to this level until they have total trust in you, and that can't happen if sex gets involved. They can dispel many of the erroneous myths men have about women perpetuated in media, songs, and of course, barber shops. Speaking of barber shops, the young man can say he picked up a good piece of advice in a barber shop about the 'Fun or Run' stages of a man's life. But we'll talk more about that later. Now before I talk about the child trap, I need to point out differences between the way things are today and the way they were back in the day.

Back in the day, there was great social stigma attached to unwed and teen pregnancy. If a woman wasn't married she didn't have kids. And if you saw a teenaged girl pushing a stroller, it was a safe bet she was babysitting or it was a sibling. It was scandalous if a woman was a grandmother and wasn't near fifty. And if a teenaged girl got pregnant, quite often she'd leave school and disappear to have the baby. Things are different now, partly because so many men have been killed in useless wars or locked up. Feminism also played a big part in the change of attitude. It's not uncommon to hear women today say they don't need a man to raise a child. And teen girls think it's the happening thing to have a baby, because they want someone to love them. I'm not making judgments mind you, I'm simply pointing out the differences in attitudes in the two eras. There were problems then, and there are more problems now. That reminds me how the Committee saved our young man from the child trap.

For the child, or for the woman?

After a sip of lemonade Uncle Question continued the story, "This trap can be set with two types of children, unborn or born. In either case tactics may differ but the weapons are always the same. The weapons are guilt, honor, responsibility and you. They always come in that order. I'm sure you already know the about 'The Unborn Child Trap' so I'm not gonna say a lot about it except to remind you that every action has a consequence. And some of the consequences out here today will kill you. So I only need say if you're gonna get wet, wear a raincoat. This will also help you to avoid the Unborn Child Trap. In some respects it is easier to avoid the Unborn Child Trap nowadays, with all the condoms available. The women in his day were heavily into the use of birth control pills. But you could never be sure if they took them. It was The Committee that saved our man from this trap."

The Cute Kid

"He met her through a relative who set up a blind date. The night of their date he picked her up at her sister's place. They had a good time, they went out again. There was a calm mystery about her that intrigued him. During their third date she skillfully maneuvered the conversation around to children. Then she told him that she had a five year old boy. That night after the date she invited him to her apartment. Following her as she went to her son's room to check on him, he looked in to see a beautiful sleeping child. Our young man immediately fell in love with this kid; he'd always liked kids. After that, the lady asked if he'd drive the baby sitter home, which he did. He couldn't, however, get the thought of that sleeping child out of his mind.

The next weekend they all went to an amusement park and our young man had a really good time, especially with the child. They did the same thing the following weekend. It was after this date that our young man casually mentioned to The Committee the woman he was currently dating. When he mentioned the child they stopped him in mid-sentence with 'What! You're dating a woman with a child?' Then they asked how he felt about the woman? He couldn't answer the questions because he'd gotten so hooked on the kid he never took the time to think about how he felt about the mother. He didn't want to do anything to hurt the child, and he felt guilty. The Committee sat him down and ran the trap down to him. After his previous experience with the string job he figured he had better listen.

Now The Committee gave our young man a nickname, Dudley. It was a take off of the cartoon character Dudley Doright. They'd tell him his actions mimicked this character. And though it was a standing joke it was in fact, a compliment. When they called him that it was usually with a smile. Not this time. They started by telling him about the things a man had to consider when dating a woman with a child. It went something like this. "First thing you'd better know is that if she's a decent woman, her child is always going to come first. This means you have to be willing to take a back seat to the child. Secondly, if she's willing to use her most precious possession to trap you she must consider you a pretty good catch. It also means she is not being honest with you. Then there's the other problem which you haven't seen yet and that is the child's father. Where is he, and what is his relationship with the woman and the child? This is a plain and simple Child Trap using G.H.R.Y.

"G.H.R.Y." he said, 'What's that?' The Chairwoman spoke saying, 'Guilt, Honor, Responsibility and You. Look at it this way. You see this child whom you like and being a good man, you feel it's not right that he doesn't have a father. This makes you feel guilty because you feel a child should have a father. And being an honorable person you feel you need to take responsibility for this role. You are the only person in this situation that you haven't considered. Look, you're a caring and considerate guy, which makes you what half the woman out here are looking for. But you're gullible and that makes you an easy target.' Then one of the other Committeewomen said, 'How do you feel about the woman? You tell us you're dating a woman and you start talking about what a great kid she has. That's what sends up the red flag for us.' "The young man hadn't thought about it like this before, but he knew they were right.

A couple of days later the woman called him about eight thirty and asked if he could come over. When he got to her place she kissed him at the door. Up until now there had been no show of affection. One thing led to another and before he knew it he was being led down the hall to her bedroom On the way, he passed the child's room He looked in and saw that beautiful sleeping child. A feeling of guilt immediately came over him. He suddenly felt unclean, like he was doing something dirty. Needless to say it was not a memorable love making session because he kept thinking about the child the whole time.

He knew she must have been faking it because he was sure his performance was not up to the usual standard. In the wee hours of the morning she snuck him back up that hallway and again he looked in at the child. That feeling of guilt came over him, only this time it was worse. If he felt dirty going up that hall, he felt positively scuzzy now coming down it. He called her a few times and finally realized he didn't really like her. He didn't tell The Committee, but he was grateful that he had these women looking out for him, even if he was too stupid to look out for himself"

After Uncle Question finished we were all back in one of those reflective silent moments again. Then Dad broke the moment saying, "Speaking of traps, this reminds me of the oldest trap of all, The Sex Trap. Many men and women have fallen for this one, only to have it end in some type of messy and antagonistic situation. This happens because they get caught up on how that person makes them feel in bed. But when that spark starts to fade, the relationship falters because they have no other common interests. They just have sex, and a relationship can't survive on sex alone. Time dulls the senses and no matter how attractive or charming a person is, after awhile it will get to be ordinary to you. Sex is just sex without a strong mutual emotional attachment." Then Uncle Question said, 'That reminds me of the time a woman tried to hook him into a sex trap."

The Sex Trap

Pouring himself another glass of lemonade, Uncle Question continued saying, "'He met her through the friend of a friend, and as with all of his first dates he gave her a flower. In those days not a lot of men gave flowers, except of course on Valentine's Day. Anyway, they'd gone out a couple of times and she found out he liked working with his hands. It was a pretty standard date and when he dropped her off at her door and thanked her for a nice evening. A couple of days later she called and asked if he could come hang a picture for her. He told her he'd just come in from playing ball but he'd come over after he cleaned up and ate. After dinner he got his tools and went to her place. During their dates she'd always been a perfect proper lady. This time it would be different. When he got to her place he wasn't prepared for...

I wonder if it's happened, to many other men?
Get asked to hang a picture, as a favor for a friend.
But when arrive to do so, it's quite another thing.
A frilly little nightie, and unbarred, dripping fangs.
My sisters tried to tell me, won't like what I was taught
Some Women are deceitful, and really do play rough.
Did she think herself so sexy, that I would lose my head?
Deceived to hang a picture, did she think I'd go to bed? My sisters
tried to tell me, it won't like what I had thought. Some women are
deceitful, not the helpless demure sorts.
Did she think me maybe desperate, or maybe I was dog Did she
think herself, so sexy, that I would lose my head? She lured me
there for unreal job, would she be real in bed? And my sisters tried
to tell me, won't like what I had thought. Some women are
deceitful, so don't you dare get caught.
It hurts because I liked her, could've been best of friends. But I
couldn't ever count on her, if I were in a pinch
And it hurts because I liked her, at least I did 'til then.
That's why I wonder if it's happened, to many other men?
Get asked to hang a picture, when it's not the real intent.
My sisters finally taught me, the lesson's finally learnt"…

We all laughed at this poem, but I knew he was serious. After things had settled down and it was quiet again Dad said, "And then there's my all-time favorite trap, The Money Trap. Again everybody broke into laughter. Then Dad and Uncle Question started going back and forth in their best falsetto voices attempting to imitate women's voices:

Dad: "Baby if you just pay it for me this month, I promise I'll pay you back."

Uncle Question: "Honey it's only a hundred and seventy five dollars and I only need it so I can look good for you."

Dad: "I'm sure you won't mind if I order two dinners, I'll eat one here and take the other in a doggie bag."

This last one had us all almost falling off our chairs with laughter, even me, because I'd had the experience. At that moment I began to feel an even deeper understanding of these men. I got a warm feeling in my chest, it felt good to be a Rhymes Man. Then Uncle Question said, 'Where was I? Oh yeah, I remember, The Money Trap."

The Money Trap

"You know if you listen, you can learn something from everybody. This was the case with our young man. He played tennis and basketball in the spring and summer and in a Touch League Football in the fall. I mentioned before he was in an on-again, off-again relationship with Ellie. Excuse me again if I stop for a moment and get back to that language thing for a moment.

In three generations the phrase that describes people living together out of wedlock has changed three times. In the sixties it was shacking-up, or shackin'. In the seventies and eighties it was called co-habitating. Now it's living together." After a pause he said, "You know, language is like life, it's always changing." Then he started back into the story.

"Our young man's living arrangement was back in the on-again phase and they'd agreed to share expenses. One day after playing basketball, he was walking back to his car. One of his friends asked him if he wanted to go get a beer. Our young man told him he didn't have any money. The friend said. 'I'll lend you some.' 'That's okay, but I couldn't afford to pay it back.' 'Wait a minute, you used to have money, what happened,' the friend asked? 'I don't know, I used to have enough money to buy beer, and now I can barely make it to the next payday.' 'That's strange' cause you are by no means extravagant, in fact folks say you're down right cheap. So how come you ain't got no money?' the friend asked. 'I've been trying to figure it out, but it just doesn't add up.'

The friend asked, 'Aren't you living with someone'? 'Yeah.' 'Isn't she helping out?' 'I guess she is.' 'You guess she is! Wait a minute, you're living with this woman and you guess she's helping out.' Talking further, he realized he was paying for everything, including rent, food and all their bills. This was why he had no money. He also realized he had no idea what she did with her money. The friend explained the possible reasons for the situation.

'Look brother, this woman is suckering you. And I don't care how good the stuff is, it's not worth goin to the poorhouse for. As I see it, there're only three reasons a woman would run a Money Trap and they're all bad. First she's tryin to get back at you or somebody else, either way you're payin. Second, she's tryin to trap you by gettin you so poor you'll have to depend on her. She can make sure you can't date anybody else because you don't have any money. And you know it takes money to date. The third reason is she just might be a leech, in which case she'll dump you when all the money's gone and move on to the next sucker. Like I said, three reasons, all bad.'

During the drive home our young man thought about all the things his friend said. He went down the list in his head and got depressed. By the time he got to his apartment he was absolutely fuming. When he got inside, the woman greeted him with, 'Hey baby, did you have a good time?' He had promised himself he was going to be cool but when he heard the words good time, he snapped. 'Good time my ass, we gotta talk!'

"Needless to say the next two weeks were very tense until she moved out. He was filled with the same kind of hate and rage that he'd felt after Love left. And, he had developed a new disgust for women. Somebody was going pay, and it wasn't going to be him. That's when the plan started to germinate in his mind. He went over all the traps he'd narrowly escaped; The String Trap, The Baby Trap, The Sex trap, and The Money Trap. God, women were a deceitful bunch, and he was going to make sure some of them pay.' Uncle Question took a sip of his drink and said "We'll get back to this later but I want to tell you about The Juggle."

The Juggle

"The juggle is a game that can be played by both men and women. Its nothing more than dating two or more people at the same time. A lot of men get into tryin to Juggle by falling back to that number one mistake, listening to other men. There're a number of reasons why a man would try to juggle. First is he might be greedy. He could be narrowing his choice of women and weighing the options; but more than likely it's an ego trip. To be able to handle more than one woman at once is a real turn-on for some men. It makes them think they're ladies men, but it's a tough game and only a certain type of man can play it successfully. Our young man tried it a few times including with woman he'd eventually marry. But he got caught each time. He'd been the juggler and the jugglee. He wasn't successful at it because juggling required two things which he wasn't good at.

The first was the ability to lie, and the second, and most important, was the ability to remember the lies. An honest person can never work the juggle very long because of the effort it takes to remember the lies, and they almost always get caught. You never want do business with anyone who's a successful juggler because you don't know when they're telling the truth. The bottom line is juggling is too stressful for the honest person. You're better off to be honest with women and tell them you're seeing other people. Let them know you're interested in getting to know them, and let them have the option as to whether or not they wish to get involved. But not all games are harmful, like the one he'd play with The Committee when they went out together. This was before the Money Trap, and the game was called, Do You wanna Sleep with us?

"As you might expect it was invented by The Committee. It was a joke but it was really a signal that it was time to leave wherever they might be on a particular night. For example, if he was with a group of guys that he didn't know, one of The Committee would come up to him and say, 'My girlfriends and I have watched you all night and we can't help ourselves, but you really turn us on. You'll have to excuse us for being so forward but do you wanna sleep with us?' She'd turned to the others, and they'd waved and smile. Then she'd lead him over to the other members and go through the fake procedure of introducing everyone, and they'd all leave together. With people's minds being what they are, anybody within earshot would think there was something freaky going on. Women would be shocked and the men stared in awe."

Sometimes You'll Fool You

After listening to this story I was thinking to myself it's a wonder that a man could ever find the right woman, with all the traps and games out there in the world. The fact it could be done was evident in the long marital history of the family. And I knew I didn't want to be the first to break the tradition. I was thinking it might be better if I didn't get married. I was pulled from the thought by Uncle Question saying, "You know most men don't deal with rejection very well. And our young man was no different. But sometimes the worst intentions turn out for the best. And he met one of the nicest women in an attempt to actually get rejected.

They met at the Chairwoman's wedding reception and purely on a lark he approached this lady. Expecting to be rejected, he introduced himself and said, 'When can you and I go out to a movie'? She thought for a second and said, I'm free next Tuesday.' This really shocked our young man because he didn't expect it, but she turned out to be one of the sweetest people you would ever want to meet. They shared a love for poetry and taking walks. And she made the best Brown Betty he'd ever tasted. Though the love and marriage thing didn't happen, they became very good friends. He learned two very important lessons from this experience. The

first was never assume anything about a woman. And second, and most important, was people in good relationships had common interests. But how was he going to find a good relationship based on trust and respect?"

Abuse of Authority

We were suddenly jerked out of the moment by the sound of a siren out on the road. After the police car passed and it was quiet again, Uncle Question said, "That police car reminds me of the problem one of The Committee members had with a policeman. Like we said before, women have some problems men never have to think about. You take the time a policeman tried to pick up one of the Committee. We'll call it Abuse of Authority.

Early one summer evening our man got a call from one of The Committee members. She'd been stopped by a cop for no reason. He threatened to give her a ticket if she didn't give him her phone number. She said she couldn't get his badge number because he hid it. Then she said she did the first thing that came to her mind and gave him the phone number of our young man. And guess who called him a few days later?" Everybody on that porch replied in unison, "The police officer." Uncle Question said, "You got it. And he was quite surprised to hear a man's voice on the phone when he asked for the lady. Our man informed the officer that the lady he was looking for was his fiancée, and that he would be willing to take a message for her. Needless to say, neither he or the Committee member ever heard from the policeman again. It just goes to show sometimes you can't trust the people you're supposed to respect."

The Fun or Run Syndrome

"Now, in that era, women were fun to be around especially women between eighteen and twenty five. They were relatively safe to go out with because they wanted to have fun. Most guys in this age range wanted the same thing. so things were cool. These women were also romantic and starry eyed. They were looking for a knight to come riding up on a white charger, and there were a lot of would-be knights driving around. This was the Fun Stage of the Fun or Run Syndrome. But in nature there is always a balance, and as the Fun Stage was a carefree time for many men, the Run Stage was just the opposite."

Then Grandpa, who'd been silent through the story spoke. "In my day, the women to watch out for were between the ages of eighteen and twenty four. With Women's Liberation and more women in the work force, the age of the dangerous woman has moved back to into the early thirties. Any man dating women in this age range would be well warned to be on alert. He should always be ready to run if he's not ready to commit.

I can't rightly say exactly what it is, but if I had to make a guess I'd say it had to do with some hormone chemical. The chemical is associated with weddings and baby showers. Apparently it only affects women between the ages of twenty six and thirty something. And it starts a clock-like ticking in their head. At twenty six or so it's kinda quiet, but as they move into their thirties it gets louder. Finally, it must sound like the chime on Big Ben because many begin getting desperate. Good men still available are forced to be constantly on the run. The ticking that these women hear is called a biological clock, and it' s during this time a lot of still available men disappear from the dating scene altogether."

Then Uncle Question said, "These men take up new interests and hobbies or go back to old ones. This was the case with our man. He got more involved with athletic activities and learning how to do new things. There was a festering sore growing in his heart which could only be filled by a woman but he couldn't trust women. The Money Trap was *the straw that broke the camels back.* It was this trap, and the events that led up to it, that caused our man to withdraw from the dating scene all together. It was also these events which began the plan for revenge on these deceitful wenches. But being a man, he loved looking at women and their bodies and the only safe way to do this was for him to watch the Go-Go dancers. This was a perfect way to fanaticize without the problems and hassles of dating. And it was while watching the dancers that the details of his plan became clear. That plan was to become The War on Women."

Chapter 12

Making Love?

"Junior, do you know the difference between having sex and making love?" I thought about this for a few seconds and I realized that I didn't, and said, 'You know, I never really thought about it, but I really don't know.' Then Dad said...

"Having sex is nothing more than a physical act, requiring no emotion. Making Love is an emotional act, coupled with a physical action."

"Women are socialized to show emotion and men aren't. Men tend to separate their emotions from their bodies. That's why you hear them talk about sex as if it were a distant action. It's why some have affairs without the guilt some women have. But society has changed and many women have been hurt and abused so often they've adapted to being like men, and can have sex without getting unemotional involved. This frightens a lot of men because they can't control them. A man that feels he needs to control a woman has issues he needs to resolve. Good relationships are based on mutual respect and acceptance. You gotta be able to accept the faults with the good. If you can't, move on and don't waste each other's time. But traditions die hard and generally, women of good moral character have difficulty separating their hearts from their bodies."

Then Uncle Question said, "If a man brags about being a great lover, there's a pretty good possibility he's not. The reason is, he's probably never taken the time to ask his partners what they preferences were. Every woman is different, and what might be a turn on for one, could be a turn off for another. You've gotta communicate your sexual requirements like everything else if you intend to have a good relationship. Our young man learned this from The Committee. They'd been hanging around together for years and talking about sex was a natural part of their conversations. You can learn an awful lot by listening. During the discussions about sex our young man listened very carefully. He rarely said anything, but he learned to be a critical listener.

I read an article a few years ago in one of your aunt's woman's magazines. The article was asking if men were taking care of business in the bedroom. It article started out saying men were getting failing grades between the sheets. Then about three quarters of the way though the article they suddenly switched tracks and said that men were doing okay in bed. It was as if they were afraid to offend their women readers by suggesting women were settling for lesser performances by their men. Listening to The Committee he learned the former was true. To listen to them tell it...

Now listen closely mister, to what we're gonna say
Love making for a woman is mostly in her mind
If you don't wanna be embarrassed,
 you've gotta take your time
And if there's something you don't know, ask before you start
They'll know you aren't very good, if you're fumbling in the dark
And do be very gentle, until they ask for more
We thought that we would tell you, there's no need to go explore

We never met a man that couldn't make love,
at least that's what they say.
But if you talk to partners, it's quite the other way.
The answers often given, should make men feel ashamed.

slam, bam, thank you mam, then off to some other dame.
They've never heard of foreplay or afterplay and,
too often it's a race, off to other place, (like sleep).
And we've heard all the bragging, of all the pipe they've laid.
It's quantity not quality, that they all seem to crave.
So if you're gonna do it, give her something she can't forget
Make her grow in anticipation until next time, you together get
We've never met a man that couldn't make love,
at least that's what they say.
But if you talk to partners, it's quite the other way.

Uncle Question continued saying, "Now we already said that our man was in the medical field in the Navy and one of his assignments was working in a nursery and delivery room This required him to learn a fair amount about female anatomy. In this process he learned about the sexual sweet spots of a woman's body. Another thing that helped him begin to understand the sexual process was a book he read while in Vietnam

"Anyone who's been in war knows it's long periods of boredom punctuated by brief periods of sheer terror and fear. It was during the boring periods our young man would read. One day someone gave him a book called 'The Kama Sutra. This book got him interested in sex as an art form. When he returned home read other books on the subject; like *The Hindu Art of Love* and *The Perfumed Garden*. And later another popular book was published called *The Joy of Sex*. As you can see he wasn't the typical man when it came to sex. He had an appreciation of the erotic arts long before Love deflowered him. With what he'd later learn about women from The Committee, he could have been dangerous. He wanted to be in love again and all it got him were hassles.

"Now let's review what's happened to our young man so far. He fell in love, got engaged and then got dumped. He got caught in a rebound situation, with a woman in a relationship that ran hot or cold. In the cold phases, he dated women who were constantly running traps and games on him. He met a group of woman called The Committee who helped him through much of this. In disgust, he stopped dating and began going to Go-Go bars. Many dancers are either gay or bisexual, he considered them safe. They had one motive, making a buck. Having a drink and spending a few bucks on a few dancers was cheaper and more hassle-free than spending a hundred dollars on flowers, dinner and entertainment only to be setup for some trap or game. Besides, one of the most beautiful things in nature is a female body in movement."

We'd come to one of those quiet moments with each of us into our private thoughts. Dad broke the silence when he got up and said, "I'm gonna get more lemonade, anyone care for some?" We all said yes, and he picked up the pitcher and went into the house. Then Grandpa got up and went to the house, leaving Uncle Question and me alone on the porch. I'd been thinking about all the things the guy in the story had gone through and I could see how he could have been very leery of women after all the traps and games. I said to Uncle Question, "The young man in the story must have been very hurt and angry after all he'd been through." Uncle Question said, "He sure was, and would later attempt to get back at women for the hurt and frustration he was feeling."

A couple of minutes later Dad came back on the porch with the lemonade. He refilled our glasses and put Grandpa's on the floor by the rocking chair. We sat in silence with our thoughts until Grandpa returned and took his seat, and Uncle Question continued the story.

Lewis Wiyd

"You know, before, we talked about how our young man declared war on women. Well, the plan for this war was formulated in the Go-Go bars. It was now the time for the plan to be executed. You gotta remember he was a nice guy, raised to be polite, courteous and respectful of others. And he had a lot of patience. He planned to use what he'd been taught growing up and what he'd learned about women from The Committee. The plan was to kill them with kindness. He'd be a perfect gentleman until they fell in love and dump them.....

Dance them, Romance them, Don't rush them, Don't trust them, Listen to what they say, Don't eye them, Deny them, Show respect in every way, Dance them, Romance them, Don't rush them, Don't trust them, Don't eye them, Deny them, Steal a her away!

"Now we talked about the rules for war and he'd use his apparent innocence for his advantage. This allowed him to sneak up on these women. And he'd use what he'd learned about watching women watch women to pick the targets...

*Can learn so much by watching,
than dealing one on one,
fighting your sexual urges,
and what they think I want.
Watching a woman watch women,
To catch what you don't see.
You learn to pay attention,
to frowns and nonchalance.
Quite often it's the tip off,
of things that you don't want
Be ere especially mindful
of envious looks to see.
For it is this that indicates,
she might be quite unique.
You'll learn so much by watching,*

than dealing one on one,
fighting your sexual urges,
and what they think I want."

Uncle Question continued the story saying, "You know life is a constant journey to find yourself. Some folks get there early and do okay. But it takes others a long time, and they gotta take a lot of bumps and bruises before they arrive. This was the case with our young man. Armed with a broken heart, good manners, a baby face and what he had learned about women from The Committee, he was ready to begin his war. And he was gonna make women pay for all those rotten things they had done to him."

Chapter 13

The War on Women

"We said earlier there were rules to this war. These rules were: a woman had to be single and totally free, which meant, no kids, husbands or boyfriends. The second rule was he could never tell a lie to mislead them. And third, if there was to be any sexual activity, the women would have to ask for it. He could in no way initiate it, not even a kiss. The targets would be only very attractive women."

Beautiful Women

Then Grandpa said, "A handsome woman has problems women of ordinary appearance don't. A lot of good men are insecure and intimidated by a beautiful woman. Many aren't self-secure enough to deal with the constant attention she gets. The guys that are left want them as arm charms or conquest to boost their ego. And we haven't even mentioned other women yet. Beautiful women have problems with other women because they happen to be born to look a certain way. Some women view other women as competition, and get upset if they don't look that good. As you can see, a beautiful woman has problems other women don't. The problems often make it appear the woman has an attitude. But really they're protecting their feelings. Then we come to the beautiful ugly. That attractive woman who knows it and thinks the world should know it too. They're so vain they're actually ugly." We all snickered, but I'd met my share of these women in college. And despite their pleasing physical appearance, their attitudes were so bad, they actually appeared undesirable.

Then Uncle Question said, "Now our young man lived across the street from one of the first women of color to really make it in the fashion business. She even made it to the cover of one of the popular news magazines. She was a pioneer, and by today's standards she'd have been a super model. When he was nineteen he came home on leave from the service. This model and her sister, who was equally good looking, took him and his best friend to New York to party. In those days the legal drinking age in New York was eighteen, and kids came from other states to drink legally. They had a great time with these older women, I say older because they were in their twenties. And every teenage boy has a fantasy about an older woman at one time or another.

Anyway, this evening was a major boost to their fragile nineteen-year old egos. Being seen with these gorgeous women was great. But they learned a valuable lesson about beautiful women, and that was they were just people with hopes and fears like anyone else. This knowledge coupled with what he'd later learn from The Committee would be useful in his war on women. He knew how to approach these women, and how to use his apparent innocence to his advantage. With patience, he was now armed to sneak up on their hearts. The battlefield would be the New York club scene, and he was ready for the seduction of a goddess...

A Seduction of a Goddess

"He picked Jen out going down the list by the numbers. He had a perfect opening after one of the player types annoyed her until she brushed him off. Quint was holding in a pent-up rage that had been festering for years. Years of carrying an unhealed broken heart, further injured by the deceptions, the traps, and the games, that rage was now about to explode. As he approached her, he took his first and last critical look at her body. From now on his focus would be on those beautiful light brown eyes and her face. So he took his last critical look at her body and made it count.

She was about five-ten with a regal posture, and she moved like a feather on a tropical breeze. Her makeup was put on in an obvious attempt to play down her features. But let's face it; if you got it, it's hard to hide. Her clothes, though not trendy for the times, were not conservative either. They fit like each stitch was made for her body alone, and what a body it was. She had a tiny waist and flaring hips which went around to a tight round rear end. He'd seen her on several occasions in the clubs on the dance floor. And he knew from her movements that she had all the right stuff in all the right places. Having watched her and having watched women watch her with envious looks, he knew she was the perfect target. Just before he reached her a guy stepped up, grabbed her arm and said, 'Hey baby, let's dance.'

She gently removed the guy's hand and said, 'Perhaps some other time.' But it wasn't what she said; it was how she said it. What she meant was, don't bother me. The guy never missed a beat, went over to next woman and did the very same thing. This time the woman agreed and they left for the dance floor. By now he'd reached her. As he stepped up next to her, he said, 'Hi I'm Quint, how are you this evening?' 'Fine thank you,' she said automatically before she'd looked at him.

When their eyes met he said, 'Perhaps you'd allow me the honor of having this dance'? Before she could answer he quickly added, 'But if now is not a good time, maybe you'd honor me with a dance later.' As she looked at him and raised her hand she gave him a smile and said, 'I'm Jen, and now would be fine.' Quint knew immediately that she had sized him up as harmless. And that's exactly what he wanted.

Thirty minutes later they left the dance floor dripping with sweat. Dancing is fun, good exercise and best of all, one of the few times you can watch a woman's body without seeming lecherous. Jen had a body that was an absolute joy to watch on a dance floor. She had the best undulating dip move he'd ever seen. Watching her do this move was like watching a snake crawl slowly across the ground. It was done with a grace which you rarely see with each body part distinctively taking its turn in the undulation. He asked if he could buy her a drink and she accepted. They went upstairs to the quiet bar and had a drink. After about fifteen minutes she excused herself to go to the powder room. As she started getting up he rose and helped her with her chair. When she returned, he rose and helped her with it again. This was an important part of his kill her with kindness routine.

For the next hour they talked, and he found out what he needed to know to plan his next move. They discussed the normal things, but most important, what she liked to do in her free time. He knew she didn't consider him datable by the fact that during the conversation she'd look away at a passing guy. Around 1:00 AM he told her he had to work that day and needed to go home and get some sleep. She said she'd lost track of time and needed to leave too. He helped her with her chair and they headed for the exit.

As they came down to the dance floor, the DJ put on a slow drag. He asked her to dance. She smiled and gave him her hand as they went out onto to the floor. This was the first time he had a chance to hold her. When he put his arms around her, he knew what he had suspected about her body was true. After the song ended they headed for the coatroom. As they were walking, he asked what clubs she liked to go to and she told him. He thanked her for allowing him to bend her ear, got his coat and left for home. Over the next month they met each other the same way five times.

She had used him on several occasions to get rid of some particularly persistent men by coming over and latching on to his arm as if he were her boyfriend. The fifth meeting was on a Friday night so they stayed out later than usual. When they were ready to leave, he asked if he could drive her home. She agreed and they headed for her place. As they got there the sun was coming up. This was the first time he had seen her in daylight. If he'd thought she was gorgeous in the dim light of the clubs, she was absolutely incredible in sunlight. She invited him in for a cup of coffee.

Once in her apartment he looked around. There were copies of famous pictures and posters covering all the walls. It was done so tastefully it did not appear to be cluttered. The living room was sparely furnished creating an open, airy feel. It was a nice place and he told her that he liked what she had done with it. She thanked him as she went into the kitchen, washed her hands and started preparing the coffee. When she finished, she excused herself saying, 'I've got to get out of these clothes,' and headed for the bedroom. He sat down at the counter separating the kitchen from the dining area and started thumbing through a magazine laying there. He was hoping this was not going to be one of those she-dog episodes. His fears were put to rest a few minutes later when she returned wearing a floor length terrycloth bathrobe and slippers.

She moved like a cat and her figure was accentuated by the movement of the robe. Every other step one of her very shapely legs would pop out from under the robe. This added an air of sexual mystery to her. Quint had seen all this from a very brief glance. Her body was seen in his periphery for the focus of his glance had been on her face; and what a face it was. Her face could have been straight out a fashion magazine. She had a clean even complexion which he liked, and when she passed going into the kitchen, he got a faint whiff of her perfume.

Opening a cabinet to get the cups, he asked if could use her bathroom She told him where it was, and when he entered he found a very neat and prim room with everything in its place. He looked at the toothbrush holder to see how many toothbrushes were in it, and saw only one. This was a first class lady. Quint felt a brief pang of guilt for what he was about to do, but the pent-up rage soon overcame that feeling. When he was finished he put the seat down, washed his hands and dried them on a guest towel He returned to his stool just as she was poring the coffee.

As he glanced down to put his spoon into the sugar bowl his glasses slid down his nose. Instinctively he reached up with a finger to push them back up and she reached across the counter with both hands and removed his glasses. She looked at him for a second and said, 'You know you're very sweet and you're kind of cute, too.' He flashed his best dimpled boyish smile' and sheepishly said, 'Thank you.' As he spooned out the sugar she watched him. In his mind at that moment he knew he had her for at long last she had finally noticed him. He had gone from a harmless nerd to sweet and cute in one fell swoop.

Lewis Wiyd

After he'd finished the coffee he said he had to go. As he got up, he put his glasses on and walked around the counter, she gently grabbed his arm with both hands to walk him to the door. At the door she thanked him for the ride home and he thanked her for the coffee. As he opened the door she gently tugged on his arm so that he was forced to bend slightly. Then she kissed him on the cheek thanking him again for the ride while at the same time handing him a small piece of paper with her phone number on it. Then she said, 'Why don't you call me sometime.' Stepping out into the hallway he put the paper in his pocket and told her he would. Thanking her again for the coffee, he turned to leave as she closed the door behind him.

A few days later he called her. During the conversation her demeanor changed, as she became more relaxed and started making jokes. By the end of the conversation they had made a date to take a walk in Central Park on the following Sunday afternoon. The same thing happened the next weekend. Each time they went out he'd bring her a flower. It was always a different kind of flower, but never roses. On their seventh date he brought her a hand written poem on parchment wrapped up with a red bow. After placing the flower in a vase she read the poem, and when she'd finished, she smiled and kissed him saying, 'You're just so sweet, where've you been all my life'? The next week they met at a club going through the routine of dancing and conversation.

When he took her home she asked if he wanted to spend the night. 'In your bed?' he asked shocked. 'No silly, I was going to give you my bed and I was going to sleep on the couch.' 'I couldn't put you out of your bed, it wouldn't be right,' he said. 'Tell you what, I'll take the couch and you take the bed.' 'Okay,' she said as she went to get him a blanket and pillow. That was the first night he slept in her apartment. She fixed breakfast as he went into her bathroom to clean up. She'd produced a toothbrush for him to use. When he was finished in the bathroom he asked, what she wanted him to do with the toothbrush? She told him to put it in the toothbrush holder. It was then that he knew that he really had her.

The following Saturday he had to work, but he called her from the job late that afternoon and they made arrangements to go dancing that night. He was to meet her at a club about ten. He didn't see her when he arrived, so he took a seat at the bar and started to listen to a spirited conversation by some of the men sitting there. A few minutes later he was startled by a pair of hands being placed over his eyes from behind. From the scent of the perfume he instinctively knew it was her. She said, 'Hello handsome, I've missed you. (He had moved from cute to handsome.) As he turned to greet her he caught a glimpse of the other men looking at her. Their glances moved from her to him and back to her again. Our man could almost hear their thoughts as they were wondering how this nerdy guy could attract such a beautiful woman.

That night, there was something different about Jen, and her dancing was a lot more suggestive. After about an hour she told him she was tired and asked if he'd take her home. Before they left she had to go to the ladies room. When she'd left him, one of the guys who had been at the bar earlier walked up to him and said, 'Brother I don't know what it is you got but you've pulled a woman that half the guys in this place have been trying to get with for months. Whatever it is you have to get a woman like that, I wish you'd put it in a bottle and give me some.' Quint didn't respond, but it did make him feel good, and when Jen returned they left.

When they got to her place she put on a pot of coffee and went to change clothes. He sat in his usual spot on the stool. Ten minutes later she returned and put her arms around him and squeezed. She went into the kitchen and took a long look at him as if trying to make a decision about something. They drank the coffee in near silence as she stared at him the whole time. Then as if a decision had been made she asked, 'Quint, do you like my body?' She stood up and did a slow turn with her hands on her hips.

Quint was caught off guard, and he had to find a non-offensive answer. He took a long look at her for the first time that she could see and finally said what The Committee would have been proud of him for saying. He said, 'I love your body, but it has to be more than just about a woman's body. Yes, I do like your body, but I like your mind more.' Her reaction was immediate, as if a big weight had been lifted from her. She did this little dance in the middle of the kitchen floor and suddenly stopped and smiled at him. Then she said, 'You'll have to excuse me, I do get silly sometimes.' She walked around the counter and into his arms giving him a passionate kiss. After the kiss she asked, 'Are you any good in bed'? 'Sure, I can sleep with best of them,' he said laughing. And this caused her to laugh too.

When she'd calmed down, she got very serious and rephrased the question, 'Are you good at making love?' He gently took her hand and led her over to the couch. After sitting down, she crossed her legs which made robe open up exposing a luscious thigh and shapely leg. She made no attempt to close the robe. Then he repeated the question, 'Am I a good lover?' As he was thinking of the answer, she said, 'Well, are you?' 'I would have to say no, but I have to explain something first.' He said, 'I've read books on the subject,' and he told her about the books he'd read. Then he said, 'As far as experience is concerned, I'm not that experienced.' Her reaction to his answer shocked him as she started laughing. His ego was instantly injured. It must have shown on his face because while still laughing she said, 'I'm not laughing at you,' she said when she'd calmed down she added, 'You're too good to be true. You must be the only man in America who will admit that he's not a good lover. That probably means you are because you're willing to learn. Any man that would read books on the subject of sex is on his way to being a great lover.' Then giving him a long serious look she said, 'Please spend the night with me.'

"Quint wanted to keep her waiting as long possible. He wanted her to the point where she was ready to tear his clothes off before giving in. But the plan was becoming more difficult by the second as he kept stealing glances at her thigh and leg. Then she asked again, 'Will you spend the night with me?' Still trying to buy time he said, 'I'll stay, but only if I can sleep on the couch.' Her answer surprised him. She just said, 'Okay baby. Is there anything I can get you in the meantime?' 'I'd like a cold glass of water, please,' he said as he stood to help her up. At that moment he thought he might have blown nearly two months time and expense by not answering her question. His mind was still on this thought when she said, 'Why don't you let me help you take off your jacket.' After she took his jacket off she hugged him. As soon her arms were around him she immediately let go and stepped back and said, 'Honey you're still all wet. Can I get you a towel or something?'

"At that point he felt positively scuzzy with his shirt sticking to his body. He said, 'First, if you would, may I please have a glass of water?' 'And second?' she asked. 'The second is, I'd like to take a shower but I don't have anything to put on when I get out.' 'That's not a problem, baby. You can wear one of my bathrobes when you get out the shower, and you can wear it when I take, I mean, put you to bed, 'she said as she quickly turned and headed for the kitchen.

As she walked across the floor humming one of her favorite songs, there was a seductive sway in her hips he hadn't seen before. After she brought him the water, she kissed him and headed toward the bedroom That sway in her hips was still there but now he had more time to look at it. When she was out of sight, he drank the water while thinking to himself how this woman really got his juices flowing. If he wasn't careful, liking her could very easily turn into love. A couple of minutes later, she returned. This time he was able to get a full frontal view of her as she walked toward him. This was the first time he'd looked at her with lust. But it was okay because she'd given him permission to do it. The long white robe accentuated every curve of her body, and with each step one of those gorgeous legs would pop out from under the robe. She was carrying three clothes hangers. When she reached him she smiled and said, 'I put a towel, washcloth and a robe in the bathroom for you. I also put a fresh bar of soap in the shower.' As he passed he kissed her and asked, 'Do you have a small paper bag?' 'Sure, under the sink in the kitchen, but what do you need it for?' 'Never mind,' he said as he got the bag. 'I'll hang up your clothes while you're in the shower,' she called after him as he headed for the bathroom...

In the bathroom, he undressed and put his clothes on the toilet seat. He put his underwear in the bag and placed it on the floor by the sink. Turning on the shower and adjusting it to lukewarm, he got in. While in the shower he fully expected that Jen would show up at any second. When it didn't happen., he thought he might still escape her bed tonight. Little did he know that this was not going to happen. When he got out of the shower his clothes had been removed from the toilet. He quickly toweled off and put on the robe. It came to just above his knees and he felt self-conscience about his skinny legs, but there was nothing he could do about it. He used the towel to wipe the condensation off the mirror. Looking down, he saw his toothbrush in the same place it had been from the first time she had given it to him. He finished brushing his teeth, folded the towel and washcloth and placed them on an empty towel rack. Looking in the mirror one final time he said to himself 'Don't lose your heart.' Picking up the bag, he stepped out into the dimly lit hallway.

Chapter 14

Making Love

When he got to the living room Jen jumped off the couch and ran into his arms. Looking down into those beautiful light brown eyes he couldn't help but tell her what he'd been thinking since the first rime he'd seen her. 'You're an incredibly beautiful woman' Smiling at him she said, 'You know, I've heard that so much I'm sick of it, but coming from you, it really feels good. Frankly, I didn't think you'd noticed.' Then she said, 'I poured you a glass of wine baby; why don't you have a drink while I shower.' Removing her self from his arms, she turned and headed toward the bedroom. He sat on the couch and placed the bag in his shoe and looked around the room.

As he picked up the glass of wine he noticed Jen had turned off all the lights except the one on the range hood of the stove. She'd put on soft music and somewhere there was the scent of candles burning. At one end of the couch was the pillow and blanket. When he saw it, he was sure he was going to escape her bed tonight. He quickly downed the wine and turned to lie down on the couch as he heard the shower go on. He spread the blanket over himself placed his head on the pillow and closed his eyes to listen to the music.

"Sometime later, his Vietnam-honed senses detected a moving presence. His eyes shot open as he turned in the direction of the movement. It was Jen walking toward him. She was wearing a floor length black negligee. He removed the blanket and sat up. She didn't come directly to him. She entered the kitchen., walked over to the counter to put the cups in the sink, then turned and walked in his direction. The sight was breathtaking for her body blocked out the direct light from the stove but it passed through the negligee showing every exquisite curve. When he saw this, he instantly knew he wasn't going to get out of her apartment tonight without giving up something, and honestly, he didn't want to.

When she reached the couch she sat in his lap and placed her arms around his neck. 'Baby, it's not right that you sleep on this couch. Look, you barely fit. Why don't you come sleep in the bed,' she said as she wiggled her hips in his lap. A part of his body took on a mind of its' own. He was quickly heading for the pure lust mode. With the last vestige of self control, he placed his arm under her legs, stood up and placed her gently on the couch.

As he sat beside her, he paused before saying, 'Are you sure you want to do this? I'm positive, it's not only something I want to do, it's what I need to do,' she said. 'Then I suppose there are some things we need to discuss, starting with what we're going to do about contraception,' he said. When they finished talking about what to do, he asked a question that would have made The Committee proud He said, 'What do you consider to be a good love making session, and how do you like to be pleasured? After listening to the question she looked at him in amazement. Seeing this, he quickly added 'How do you turn a person on if you don't know what turns them on.' She thought for a second and quickly took control of the situation by saying, 'Perhaps I should show you. '

An Hour Later...

When the kiss ended, she... He was thinking...
She's not going to?
She's not going?
She's not?
She's?

Oh My God !!!

Insatiable

"He was awakened by a ray of sunlight beaming directly onto his face through a crack in the drapes. He didn't know what time it was but, as he became fully conscious, he was sure it was early morning. He knew he could not get back to sleep so he started to get up. As he slowly sat up he glanced over at Jen who was still asleep on her back under the sheet. There was a lock of hair across her face and her mouth was turned up in a slight smile. There was no need to wonder if she'd been satisfied, one look at her and the answer was obvious. He slowly got up from the bed feeling very weak. Looking around the room, he noticed the candles had burned out and there was the slight scent of candle wax in the room Picking up the robe from the floor, he quietly left the bedroom closing the door behind him His first inclination was to get dressed and go home, but The Committee had taught him that many women wanted the men to be there when they woke up. So, he decided to stay at least until she was awake.

He went to the kitchen, washed his hands and put on a pot of coffee. Then he went into the bathroom Fifteen minutes later he emerged from the bathroom having showered and brushed his teeth. He was famished so he went in the kitchen and opened the refrigerator. He took out four eggs, some bacon and some cheddar cheese. He found a large pan and quietly placed it on the stove and turned on the gas. He opened the bacon and put a few strips in the pan. While he was turning it over there was a noise in the hallway. Turning down the gas, he walked over to the front door and looked out the peephole. There was no one in sight, but there was a New York Times lying on the floor in front of the door. He opened the door, picked up the paper and stepped back inside. Closing the door, he went back to the kitchen. As he removed the bacon from the pan, there was a stirring noise coming from the bedroom. The door opened, Jen stepped out and called 'Good morning, baby.' 'Good morning,' he said as she entered the bathroom and closed the door.

"Fifteen minutes later she came out of the bathroom and, walking up behind him, she put her arms around his waist and squeezed. She walked around the counter, picked up a cup, poured herself a cup of coffee and sat down on the stool on which he usually sat. He whipped the eggs and poured them into the pan while pushing down the handle of the toaster. He opened the cabinet and took out two plates. The eggs and toast were ready at the same time. Half an hour later they had finished breakfast."

Uncle Question paused and took a sip of his lemonade. I had gotten so engrossed in the story that I almost forgot that I had to go to bathroom, and this pause was a perfect opportunity to go. Standing up I said, 'I've got to go, but don't tell any more of the story until I get back.' They all looked at me and smiled as I went into the house. As I was passing the kitchen on the way to the bathroom I looked in and the room was almost full of women. I hurried to the bathroom and fortunately it was empty. When I came out Grandma was standing by the kitchen door with a plate of fresh baked cookies. 'Junior would you please take these cookies on out with you,' she said. I took the plate and thanked her, as. I headed back to my seat. On the porch I passed the plate of cookies to Grandpa. He offered everybody some, and we all took one. We sat for a minute or so in silence eating cookies and drinking the lemonade, Then Uncle Question continued the story saying…

"Quint had just finished washing the dishes and was wiping down the stove and counters when he suddenly got the feeling that he was being stared at. Turning around he saw Jen looking at him with a smile on her face. 'I see you know your way around a kitchen,' she said. 'Where did you learn that?' 'In my family, before you leave home you have to learn how to do a few basic things.' 'Like what,?' she said. 'Things like how to wash, iron, sew on buttons, and most importantly how to cook,' he said. 'I see you learned your lessons well, especially the cooking part, that breakfast was good,' she said. 'And speaking of cooking, you really were cooking last night. I really want to thank you. You were incredible,' she said with a devilish smile. 'And you were too,' he said. 'I thought you were trying to kill me.' 'Quint baby, you have to understand I haven't made love in a very long time. When you've waited that long, you kinda get carried away, especially if it's good.' Then she got very serious and said, 'Baby I don't want you to have the wrong impression of me, but some of the things we did last night I've never done with anyone else, ever.' 'Likewise' he said. 'Women don't take me very seriously. They think I'm a kid and want to play games with me. All I seem to ever get out of these games are hurt feelings.' 'Baby, I would never play games with you, and as far as those other women are concerned, it's their loss,' she said, as she came around the counter and hugged him.

While she was still in his arms she said, 'I love the way you hold me; you're so gentle. I knew that the first time we danced close. You're so different from the guys I usually met (met, past tense, he thought). 'They're always in such a rush, and you don't seem to be in a hurry to do anything. I've wanted to go to bed with you for the last two weeks. It was so bad it almost hurt, so Thursday I bought the negligee and decided I was going to seduce you. I thought I'd get you to work up a sweat at the club and bring you back here. That would have made you feel you needed to take a shower. Once you were in the shower, I was planning to come in take advantage of you. When we got here last night, I started to feel guilty.

I thought about the first time we met and you asked me to dance. I mean really asked me, most guys ask with words and tell with actions. But you actually asked. (Chalk up another one for The Committee, he thought). Then I thought about the times we'd gone out and you never assumed anything. You always asked permission first. That's when I realized I hadn't given you permission to look at my body. Do you know that before last night, I'd never seen or felt you look at my body? And then I gave you permission and you did. I saw the lust in your eyes and I wanted you to lust for me. It felt good because it was the first time in my whole life that I've ever had control of when and how a man looked at me. Everything worked out, but for all the right reasons. Something else you should know, I would have slept with you the first night you stayed here if you'd have asked. But I know it wouldn't have been as good as it was last night." Suddenly, her face turned sad and a tear came to her eye. Then she said 'I'm sorry I tried to deceive you baby, it will never happen again. '

"Quint could have easily fallen in love with her at that very moment, but his mind focused on the word deceive, and his heart frosted. He said, 'That's okay baby, no harm done,' as he brushed the tear away and kissed her on the forehead. She buried her head in his chest as she said, 'You're too good to true.' Then she broke into a smile and kissed him. He was about to tell her he had to go, when she said, 'Would you like some dessert?' 'At eleven in the morning,' he asked? 'That's not the type of dessert I had in mind,' she said with that devilish smile. She then let her robe fall to the floor as she did a grind against him. His reaction was immediate, and she knew it as she took his hand and started to lead him toward the bedroom. 'I'm too tired to do this,' he protested. 'That's okay, baby, you won't have to do a thing. I'll do all the work.'

He was awakened by a feeling he was being stared at. Opening his eyes he found Jen laying across the bed with her chin propped in both hands looking at him. Smiling, she said, 'Good afternoon, sleepyhead.' He could tell from the position of the sun that it was late afternoon, so he said, 'Good afternoon.' He rolled out of the bed and went into the bathroom. Quint and the lady were together every night for the next week, and she would always find a way to get him in bed. He was almost at his limit for sex, but he still hadn't heard those three little words that would declare the battle officially over. Those words were, I Love You. He thought he would hear these words some night in the heat of passion. That was why he put his body through the stress of too much sex, but it wouldn't happen that way."

Pussy Whipped

"When he got home from one of those grueling Friday night/Saturday morning sessions, it was three in the afternoon and he barely had the strength to take off his shoes. He fell on the bed fully dressed and immediately fell into a deep sleep. He awoke to the ringing telephone, and when he looked at the clock, it was a quarter to eight. When he answered the phone it was The Chairwoman, 'Where you been? We haven't heard from you in some time. I know you're not back with that woman again, so it must be something new.' 'Maybe,' he said. 'Why don't you come on over, we've got crabs, shrimp and I made Gumbo.' If it hadn't been for the fact that he hadn't eaten since breakfast he would have stayed home and slept. He told The Chairwoman he'd be there in thirty minutes. Then he showered, dressed and went to meet The Committee.

When he got to her house and they saw him, they knew something was up because he looked drained. They had been looking at him for years and knew when things weren't right with him. One of them said, 'We haven't seen or heard from you in two weeks and that's not like you, so what's up?' 'Nothin,' he said. 'Then maybe you should go see a doctor 'cause you look like somethin' the cat dragged in.' 'Cat, that's it, Dudley is pussy whipped,' one of them said. They all laughed. (He made a mental note, not to spend so much time around these women, because they knew him too well) 'Okay, what gives Dudley?' one of them said.

"The first question asked was, 'How long has it been since you've had a full nights sleep?' He knew the grilling had started and he was in no mood to fight them. Besides, he could never win these things with them anyway. They always ended up with information they wanted. So he said, 'Seven nights.' 'One week!' they all said at once. 'And how many hours of sleep have you had in those seven days?' another one asked. 'I don't know, maybe twenty hours or so,' he said. 'Twenty hours of sleep in seven days! Fool, are you on some kind of ego trip, or do you think you're superman? You can't work all day and screw all night and maintain your health. That's why you look like something the cat dragged in. You know, there's no world record for orgasms so why are you trying to set one,' the Chairwoman asked? 'The world is full of graves of men who screwed themselves to death. The bottom line is, she's got you pussy whipped figuratively and literally. '

'There are only three reasons a woman would try to pussy whip a man. The first is she may be a nymphomaniac which is rare. The second is she hasn't had any in a long time, but seven days of all night sessions seems a little excessive; two or three all-nighters should have satisfied that craving. That brings us to the third reason, which is probably the case here. The woman probably has very strong feelings for you, but she doesn't want to be the first to say the magic words, so she's trying to make you say it in the heat of passion. Another part to this angle is if she beats you up enough there will be no way you're gonna be able to give it to any other woman. Believe me, I know, I've been there. You do know you can tell her you've had enough?' He was shocked because she had the situation exactly right, but it was he who wanted to hear the magic words during sex and it was killing him. At that point, he went home to get some sleep.

"During the drive home, the words of his Grandmother suddenly jumped into his mind, 'She can look up longer than you can look down.' He thought about what The Chairwoman said about his ego. He hadn't thought about it from this perspective, but he had to admit that it had been his ego that made him think he could screw Jen into submission. Now that he knew this wasn't going to happen, he was resolved to the fact that he was going to have tell her he wasn't able to deal with all the sex. Little did he know, Mother Nature was going to help him get the much needed rest he needed. The help came in the form of a twenty-eight day cycle. "

Thank God for Periods

"He called Jen the next day and she told him she'd be out of commission a few days because she had a 'visitor'. He apologized for having been over zealous in bed and she said she'd enjoyed every moment. Then she told him that maybe she'd gotten a little carried away herself and from that point on it would be different. Somehow he knew it would be. He called her on Wednesday and she asked if he was coming over because she needed a hug. He picked up some Chinese food and they had dinner together.

After dinner they sat on the couch and she curled up in his arms. He actually thought about them with a house and family. He could have easily fallen in love with her. She was everything he ever thought he wanted in a woman. She was considerate, compassionate, smart, funny, sexy, and beautiful, what more could a man ask for? That night was the first that they slept together in her bed without making love, and she maintained a body contact with him the entire night. The next morning they got up early because he had to cross the river to go to work. After breakfast when he was ready to leave, she kissed him at the door and asked if he'd come over for dinner, and he agreed.

That night, he showed up with a bottle of her favorite wine and a dozen yellow roses. They had a beautiful candlelit dinner after which they sat on the couch. During one point in the conversation she looked at him and said, 'You know, I could easily fall for you.' He told her he could fall for her, too. Then she asked him where the relationship was going? And he told her he didn't know. That night ended the same way it had the previous night, as did the one that followed."

The Tease

"On Saturday they were back to their routine of dancing and conversation. While they were dancing to a slow song, Jen started making sexual suggestions which was a side of her he'd never seen before. She'd always been the perfect classy lady. If he thought this was a different side of her, he'd soon find out it was going to get even more interesting. As they were leaving the dance floor, Jen took a look at the bar. A devilish smile came across her face as she said to him, 'Do you want to help me have some fun?' 'Sure, I'm game,' he said. He had no idea what she had in mind, but from the devilish smile he knew it was going to be a doozy. Then she said, 'Don't look now, but when you get a chance take a look at the three guys at the far end of the bar. And then watch the parade of women trying to get their attention.'

Quint took a casual look toward the bar and saw the men. Two of them were leaning on the bar like Joe Cool; the third was sitting on the stool between them with his back to the bar. They were all good looking men and they knew it. They were surveying the women like they were standing on a hill looking into a valley of flowers deciding which ones to pick. The women would casually pass in ones and twos, smile at them and speak. The guys would nod and say hello while continuing to search for hot prospects. When our man had taken all this in, he said to Jen, 'I've got it.' Then she said 'Now let's have some fun. Those guys are hounds and they've been pestering me for months. It's time for some payback.' Then she said, 'Let me see your watch. I'm going to the ladies room, but in exactly twenty minutes I want you to meet me at the bar.'

'I want you to say the most vulgar thing you can think of' As Quint was about to protest she said, 'You're a veteran, I know you can do it. Remember, exactly twenty minutes. That should give them enough time to get pretty well lathered up. The twenty minutes starts now,' she said as she headed for the ladies room looking at her watch. Quint now knew what she had in mind from her last statement and slowly moved to a position where he could watch what was about to happen.

Ten minutes later he saw Jen approach the bar. The guys all but fell over themselves to make room for her. The guy on the stool got up and offered her a seat. Almost in unison, their hands went up to signal the bartender for a drink. Though he couldn't hear any of the conversation, he could tell by their gestures they were squabbling over who was going to buy her the drink. Then Jen said something and they all calmed down. Quint turned to look at the other women's reaction to all of this. A few of them were shooting contemptuous dagger stares at her. He had just gotten a practical lesson as to the problems she must have had in her life because of her looks. With five minutes left on the clock, Quint slowly circumnavigated the room He had judged the distance and figured how long it would take to get to the bar at the designated time. He also noticed that the men had all of a sudden gotten closer to her so that they almost completely hid her from view.

Quint got to the bar and as he came up behind them he said, 'Hey baby you wanna go home and fuck?' Right at that moment Jen was saying, 'And here he is now' as she turned around, smiled gave him a wink. The guys all turned at once and looked at him. As Jen got off the bar stool, she grabbed Quint's arm, turned back to the men and said, 'I do want to thank you gentlemen for the champagne; it's been stimulating. You all have a good night.' The guys mouths fell open at the same time their eyes focused on Quint. Before they could react, Jen led Quint towards the coat room As they were turning to leave, Quint got a quick glimpse of the bar. On the bar were three opened bottles of Champagne. When they were out of earshot of the guys at the bar, she said, 'Your timing was perfect as always,' giving him that devilish smile."

Confessions in a Car

"Outside, she broke into hysterical laughter. After she calmed down a little she said, 'God, that was fun, I've been wanting to do that for a long time.' She was still giggling to herself as they reached the car. During the drive to her place he told her what she'd done wasn't nice. Then he thought about it and realized he didn't know what she'd done since he was across the room while all this was going on. So he said, 'That baby, was teasing.' Before he could speak again, she said, 'Look, baby, what I did tonight, I did for two reasons.

The first reason was that those guys have been bugging me for months. They're pure dogs and they needed to be taught a lesson. Hell, between the three of them they've probably screwed half of New York. But the real reason I did it was for you. I needed you to see that I can have any man I want. It's not conceit, it's something I've always had. But I didn't choose you. It was something that just happened and now I know that it was never about choosing or making it happen. It's about letting it happen. With you, I never needed to put up any defense or look for an alternate motive. I was always taught not take advantage of people, and when you look like I do, it can be a very easy thing to do. I have problems on my job for no other reason than the way I look. I have very few girlfriends for the same reason. I was lonely and you've given me what I've needed more than anything, a friend. You've been the best friend I've had since I was a little girl. And I don't want to do anything to mess that up. I'd always thought I was a good person, but I was starting to have doubts. Since I met you, I actually like myself. You slowed my life down so I could look at it. Now that I've seen it, I can deal with it.' Then there was silence.

When they arrived at her apartment, she turned and hugged him. She held on to him for quite awhile and when she finally let go she said to him, 'Thank you for being my friend.' This woman could melt his heart and every time he closed it, she'd open it again. The confessions in the car had given him a new perspective on the problems of being physically attractive. Add to this the problems of being a woman, working in a traditional man's job, he could see why she was the incredibly strong woman she was. He already respected her but now he admired her. To him, she was now a hero. His definition of a hero was not that once in a life time action in a critical situation, but rather the individual that did extremely difficult tasks routinely, and Jen was a hero. He wondered if he'd be an asset or a liability for her if the relationship progressed. He was broken from his thoughts by a kiss. The love making that night was nothing short of incredible. Starting with a shower together, and him giving her a massage, which created a new interest for him, but we'll talk more about this later."

Vapors

'The next morning at breakfast they were going through the paper and Jen saw an announcement for an art exhibition. She told him she'd like to see it, so they went. They were walking through the exhibit arm in arm, and were almost at the end, when Jen stepped in front of him and hugged him. Looking up at him with those beautiful eyes she said... "I love you" and kissed him. Who would have thought he'd win the battle in a museum standing in front of a Monet. He didn't say anything, just smiled. He figured Jen must have thought it was because he was happy to hear the words, but she could not know it was because he had won the battle. That evening when they got back to the apartment he walked her to the door and told her he couldn't stay because he had some things to do. She said, 'That's okay baby, you do what you have to do, I'll talk to you later. She kissed him and closed the apartment door. He never saw her again! As he drove away from her apartment for the last time, he thought to himself if she'd waited another day he'd have married her. He wooed her for months before he'd finally won the battle. "

Notches on the Belt

"Aleata and Cleo were not much of a challenge after Jen. Aleata lost the battle in a month, and Cleo gave in a day short of a month. Collectively, they weren't half the woman Jen was. It seemed that their only goal in life was to find a guy and settle down. Beyond this, they had no concrete plans for the future or more importantly for themselves. The only thing that could said about them was they looked good and that was sure to fade with time. After Cleo, Quint started the search for the next target. But he had a nagging regret about Jen which lasted for many years. While he was searching for the next target, he had an encounter with another woman which was to him nothing more than something to do." When Uncle

Question got to this point in the story he said, "It's my turn to go to the little boy's room" He excused himself and went into the house while the rest of us sat quietly and listened to the sounds of the approaching night.

Something to Do

When Uncle Question returned he sat down, took a sip of his drink and immediately got back into the story saying, "Where was I? Oh yeah, I was talking about something to do.

You know there's a saying, 'Don't shit where you eat.' It means you should try to avoid relational entanglements with people in constant proximity. This means on your job or where you live. Quint didn't heed this advice even though he'd heard the maxim. He'd always helped his neighbors whenever he could and was always being asked to do things or assemble something. When it snowed, all the able bodied folks in the apartment would turn out in the parking lot to shovel out the cars after the snow plow went through. It was the closest the complex ever came to a party, and it was during one of these snow parties that this started.

As I said before, he was courteous. One of his neighbors, a woman, would play the helpless female role for all it was worth. And she played the role after a particularly heavy snow storm. It was a Saturday morning, and after the plow went through, the parking lot was full of people shoveling. Everyone was helping each other shovel out their cars. By eleven o'clock they'd finished, and folks headed back to their units. Quint was one of the last to leave when this woman came out. She started the helpless female bit, acting like she didn't know how to use a snow brush or shovel. And he ended up cleaning her car. When he'd finished, she thanked him and told him she'd been having stiffness in her back and shoulders. When he mentioned he did massages and was working toward a license, she suggested maybe he could come and give her one. He told her he was too tired but if she called him later he'd see what he could do. He went back to his apartment showered, ate and went back to bed."

Now I have to tell you about this woman," Uncle Question said, "She was one of those prissy people, always in the latest fashions and very superficial. Perhaps vain would be a better word. One day he got home from work and didn't feel like cooking. He decided he'd go out to eat, but he didn't want to go alone. He called The Committee but no one was available. He was about to give up on the idea when he remembered he left his briefcase in the car. When he went out to get it he ran into this neighbor taking groceries out of her car. 'A gentleman always offers to help a lady,' so he offered to help, and she accepted.

After he had taken her bags to the apartment and before he thought about it he said, 'Would you like to get something to eat?' Before he could think of a way to retract the offer, she'd accepted. And just like that he was committed to taking her to dinner. He'd always thought she was less than real, but she could hold a decent conversation so it wasn't as bad as it could have been. When they returned he thanked her for going and went home. The next day she called to thank him again for the dinner. He told her it wasn't a problem and they ended the call He didn't think anymore about it and they never got together again until the night after that snowstorm

'After dinner that night, he was watching TV when the woman called. She asked when he was going to give her the massage he'd promised. He knew he hadn't promised anything, but since he needed the practice, he went anyway. After the massage, he was preparing to leave when she stepped in front of him and kissed him. She told him she wanted to thank him for all the nice things he had done for her. He protested strenuously but she wouldn't take no for an answer. Perhaps I can say it better this way...

Everybody knows one, or maybe quite a few.
 A woman who thinks she's all that,
and better than me and you.
Can easily spot her in high fashion clothes,
with that much too exaggerated walk.
And no matter in what setting,
  speaks that much too proper talk.
Watch other women watch her,
 then talk with snide remarks.
When all these things would happen,
inside his head, a bell goes off.
You know that he has found her,
this queen of material things.
His plan is very simple to get over on,
 the incomparable Miss Thang.
For she's an easy target,
 with her haughty arrogance.
Though she's not hard to look at,
she can't seem to keep a man.
There must be something wrong with them,
those endless one-night stands.
A legend in her own mind
 never doing for others a meaningful good.
She 'is lonely, and thinks the world is jealous
 of her superior attitude.
Becomes an easy mark for any man,
just wanting something else to do.

Lewis Wiyd

In every sentence that she speaks contains the words 'I am'
She's so wrapped up in vanity,
 he need only follow one simple plan.
Just tell her what she wants to hear,
 and she's on you like a tan.
So in the morning after, when all the truths are told,
 believes that thing between her legs, is purist of the gold.
As man should be forever grateful,
 That on him, her favors she bestowed.
But she herself has ne'er examined,
 the reason the phone it never rang.
And now she is mad with every man,
 because another one got over on,
The incomparable Miss Thang...

Quint was winning battles in the war, but wasn't as happy about the victories as he thought he'd be; and he had one regret, Jen. He wasn't sorry he'd left her, but it was the cowardly way he'd done it. And there was no honor in that. He told himself he was getting soft and he needed to be less of a punk. He was out on a target evaluation search one night when he ran into that tall version of Love in the bar we mentioned earlier. It was meeting her and other events, that made him take a hard look at himself and his life. He remembered hearing a friend Ollie say, 'You know, a man can't begin to grow until he looks in the mirror and admits to himself he's just a dog.' He knew he had finally reached the point where he have to look in that mirror. "

Man to God, Man to Woman

If I came from you, If I derive my strength from you,
Why do I try so hard to callous my heart,
 And break, yours?

"Its unfortunate women have made a good man to go to these extreme measures, but until you confront that first love you can not begin to heal. You respect women, but you don't like them very much."

Lewis Wiyd

Chapter 15

Looking In the Mirror

Critical Events

"Looking back at his life over the last few years, Quint realized Tina, the woman in the bar, had taught him a very valuable lesson about misplaced anger. He had toyed with women's feeling and broken hearts. At the same time this was going on, one of the Committee members was dealing with a bad relationship. A couple of days later the war ended when she called crying...

She called me crying on the phone.
Said I was the only one home.
Could barely make out through the sobs
How some guy had just broken her heart
Said she'd tried to show him she cared,
He dispelled the defense of her fears.
As he said all the things she would hear.
For he was a true gentleman see,
She thought was the man of her dreams.
Turns out was a wolf dressed like sheep,
and all he wanted was a piece.
Cause in bed, he declared he was good.
His opinion was not understood.
When they got to doin' the do
As she was beginning, he was through.
Now tell me, to her what could I. say?
When the man she described, it was me.
I could never be that man again,
A good man don't screw over a friend...

Uncle Question took another sip of lemonade and continued the story saying. "A few days later while Quint was getting ready to go to work he looked in the mirror. He didn't like the face staring back at him. He was a dog and it was at this point he decided he was going to change. He resolved never to continue doing the things he had done to women. He thought about Jen and said aloud to himself: 'Jen, I'm sorry for what I did to you. You didn't deserve it.' He felt better but he knew he could never face her again. He would pray for God's forgiveness and put it in His hands, which is what he did. He was a new man and could now begin to love himself. Just like that his life had changed, and he'd had finally accepted himself for what he was, a caring and loving person. This would never change the fact people would always try to change him. And he'd spent much of his life trying to please other people. But at long last, he had accepted himself and to hell with those people that couldn't deal with it.

Quint was now back on a fairly even keel He was approaching the time when a lot of the women he dated were approaching that dangerous desperate age when they felt a strong desire to land a husband. As a result, he was wary of all women. The only women he trusted were The Committee, and he spent much of his time with them. Since most of his male friends were married he was out by himself He was constantly encountering desperate women and he even tried a long distance romance which ended with the same ultimatum. 'the women's games were getting more subtle, and many tried to convince him with everything they had, that they were perfect for him. It seemed the new prevailing tactic was to keep a man waiting as long as possible before any physical contact. This added to the expense as well as the anticipation, which could be a trap all its own."

The Call

"One day Quint got a phone call, and to his shock it was Love. When he heard her voice, memories long since buried came rushing back. She said she wanted to see him and was at her brother's house. It had been seven years, and he was both excited and apprehensive about seeing her. After all those years, he wondered why she wanted to see him. When he got to the house he had to remind himself not to look at her eyes too long. He knew they had a power over him and he didn't think that he could handle it. The next thing he knew, he was ringing the door bell

She answered the door and right away made him feel comfortable. It was something she'd always been able to do from the very first time they went out. They spent about a half hour together and he had a nagging feeling that she wanted to tell him something. During the conversation, he was so busy protecting his heart he was afraid he would say something embarrassing. When the visit was almost over, he felt comfortable enough to take a long look at her. She was more beautiful than ever been. And at that moment he realized he still loved her. But it was different now; it wasn't the raging passion driven love it had once been. It had matured and grown to a comfortable mellow kind of thing. It was kinda like a pair of well worn slippers for the heart; it fit perfectly. By the time he left, he felt like he was floating on a cloud. He told himself if he ever got another chance, he would never let her get away again. As it happened, the next time he saw her was four years later under very different circumstances.

The Committee continued to lead him past the traps. He was still in that on-again off-again arrangement and knew very soon he would have to make a decision about what he was going to do about it. He began to understand it wasn't love that kept him in this arrangement; it was guilt disguised in comfort. In those days, those in the alternative lifestyle weren't coming out. And he began to suspect this woman had some of these issues.

Was in a weaker moment and fell in love with love,
And you were there and became the object of my emotion.
But now I question daily, if I really do love you?
Or if it's really nothing more, than I got used to you?
Now I don't have the courage to start another quest,
I'm comfortable when you're around, I'm used to you I guess.
Remember when I met you, I tingled from your touch,
And now I question daily why, I'm used to you I guess.
Who wants new hassles really, I got past those with you.
The answer comes quite clearly, I just got used to you.
It's funny how romantic love, departs so rapidly.
But is this really true to all, or unique to you and me?
For in a weaker moment, I fell in love with love,
Got comfortable with you around, Got used to you I guess...

Once again Quint retreated to the safety of the Go-Go bars. He figured there were three reasons men went to these places. The first was guys liked to look at the girls. Second, some guys went to avoid the hassle and expense of dating. Then there's the married guy who goes to get a break from the routine of married home life. There's also a tremendous amount of business conducted in these bars. In a way its like a poor man's golf course. Quint learned about drudgery of married life listening to married men talk. He soon tired of this scene and was now sure he wouldn't ever run into the elusive Miss Right. He'd long since given up on looking for love when he made the discovery.

It seems that I should know by now,
not let my heart so easily fly,
To those who hold so little stake,
and with my feelings frivolously play.
And in my life some loves I've had
and woefully they've turned out bad.
No longer shall I be a fool
* so painful, oh this golden rule,*
But what is life that I should live,
* if I have not a heart to give?*
Some say insane and I may be,
though other fools chase destiny.
For as will tick loves endless clock,
* if I in pain wait long enough,*
To keep the faith in love passed time,
before 'tis done I'll sure find mine.
And in my mind some theories change,
but there's one that still remains.
Like what is life that I should care,
if I had not a love to share.
As moon so oft affect the tide,
tis often best to swallow pride,
And err remember this lament,
from hell all loneliness is sent.
I may be wrong I may be not,
but gather in this minute thought,
To lose loves' faith is but just to die,
and not in graves do all dead lie.
In closing now I do resolve,
to mope does not the problem solve,
So gather up your shattered heart
* and once again do make a start,*
For what is life that one should live,
if one has not more love to give...

Lewis Wiyd

Chapter 16

The Discovery - Miss Right

Finding Miss right Is the ultimate paradoxical experience, because You can't find what you're looking for until you find yourself...

It was getting dark, as the last visible rays of sun were quickly falling behind the hills, and the crickets were in full song. Uncle Question was eating his last cookie. By now, I was so engrossed in the story I couldn't wait to find out what happened next. Uncle Question took another sip of the drink, and continued, "I was saying, our man had just about given up on finding Miss Right. He'd been through the dating wars and had the scars to prove it. He found he was spending more time in the kitchen of The Chairwoman. She was now married and he had to call before going to her house. It was a Saturday afternoon and some of The Committee members were sitting in the kitchen. There was music on the stereo and no one was saying anything. They were just kinda hanging out.

Sitting in silence, his eyes slowly moved from one member to another as they stared into space, listening to the music. That's when he saw her, I mean, he really saw her. It was as if he was seeing her for the first time even though they'd been friends for years. They'd gone out a few times over the years, but she was like a sister to him. She'd had her own relationship for years just like he had. Quite often she'd be missing when the group went out together. Their lives paralleled each others to the point that the same things happened to them at the same time. She was raised with the same kind of values as he had, and their families had known each other for years. She was a conservative, proper lady and Quint thought she might even be a bit boring. But while she was sitting across from him looking down at the floor, he finally noticed her. At that moment he realized to his surprise, she was what he had been looking for all his life. And, he didn't have to search for her because she'd been there the whole time. It's just that he'd never really seen her before. He didn't say anything out of the ordinary at that time, but during the drive home he thought about her.

On the way home he decided to head for the place he always went when he needed to clear his head and sort things out; he went the beach. He'd always loved the ocean and the things related to it. While walking on the beach he took a long look at his life. He thought about Love, Jen and the traps, games, and deceptions women had been trying to run on him. He thought about how futile his attempted revenge had been. His thoughts went back to the woman from The Committee. He didn't trust any women other than The Committee. And now, anytime he dated anyone he was always looking for the trap. He instinctively knew she'd never do that since she had actually helped guide him past some of the traps. She was a good friend, but he still thought of her as a sister. After awhile, he pushed the thoughts about her to the back of his mind and went home.

A few days later he was sitting in The Chairwoman's kitchen listening to music They were alone in the house and he was kinda verbalizing his thoughts. He really had no intention of mentioning a certain Committee Member, it just sorta slipped out. Realizing what he said, he immediately tried to cover it up. When that didn't work, he told The Chairwoman she had to keep their conversation a secret. She

Lewis Wiyd

told him she thought they were perfect for each other and challenged him to do something about the situation within a specified period of time or she was going to spill the beans. As you can imagine, this put him in a mental bind.

Quint thought a lot about this woman. His fantasies were not the lustful kind, but the kind where they were walking together on a tropical beach. She never teased him like the other members of The Committee and the only indication that she might be interested in him was the one time he pulled one of his visual teases on The Committee - he had caught her stealing glances at him. Other than that, he figured he was barking up the wrong tree. He always thought of her as a sister and to him, that was the problem. Quint was being squeezed between this dilemma and the time constraint of The Chairwoman. One day before the deadline, he asked her out but he suspected The Chairwoman had already told her. The date wasn't too bad because they had a lot in common. Needless to say, their relationship' progressed to the point where he began to think of her constantly.

As you might have expected, Quint had been through so much he'd developed an automatic resistance to getting involved with a woman. Even now, it kicked in and he was still fighting. He was looking for the, but, which up until now had always sprung up in all his relationships. And he was still dealing with the sister-thing. Unlike the others, this lady handled him gently and with a lot of patience. She never pushed him into anything and never tried to change him. He'd developed a paranoia which strengthened his resistance and protected his heart.

Quint was slowly falling in love and didn't know it. While he still had a nagging urge to flee, The Committee did their part gently pushing him in the right direction. You know, Junior, men don't fall in love, they jump in. But when you jump in too often and you get burned enough, you get weary of love, and you get cynical. Make no mistake about it, you will fall in love and you will have your heart broken. How and with whom you recover from this determines how soon you can get on with the rest of your life. Even though it had been ten years, Quint was still recovering from his first love experience. It was a series of traumatic events; however, that caused a deeper bond between him and this lady.

Death and Crisis

"First a good friend died, then he hit one of those crisis points in his life. He had not yet reached any of the major goals he had set for himself. One Saturday afternoon they were in his apartment when all this came down on him. He was emotionally broken, and she was there to hold him and tell it would be okay. That's when he knew he had to stop taking life for granted. He'd been at his lowest point, and she had been there help him though it. After that he never looked at her as a sister again. His views about her were changing and his thoughts were now centered on what he was feeling for her, but he wasn't quite sure if it was love. One day he realized that this was the real thing and the search was over. And it wasn't until he stopped looking that he found her.

Their relationship took a new and better direction. It was love, and it was based on years of friendship, understanding and respect. They had a lot in common and he could talk to her about anything. Most important he felt comfortable enough with her to say how he felt. Often, they'd say the same thing at the same time. But he was still hesitant to commit until. an event we'll call the fly on the wall.

The Fly on the Wall

I could barely make out the shapes in the dark as Uncle Question continued saying, "I was talking about the fly on the wall. Remember I said before when it came to relationships, women are smarter than men. The reason for this is because women are generally more observant. When a woman is really into a man she will study everything about him. She'll watch his expressions, his movements and even the way he looks when he's sleeping. Because of this, they tend to be one step ahead of their men in relationships. Quint was about to get an up close and personal look at the validity of what The Committee had been saying for years.

Now the Committee told Quint about this but he'd never got a practical look at it until that fateful Saturday at The Chairwoman's house. When he arrived, The Chairwoman and another friend were in the kitchen playing Backgammon. Their husbands were in the back bedroom. After saying hello, he went back to the bedroom. The husbands were concocting a plan to go out for the evening without the wives. They were trying to come up with a plan they thought the women would go for. After listening to this for a while, Quint went back into the kitchen, sat down and watched the women play the game.

Quietly The Chairwoman said to her friend, 'They're trying to get out.' 'Yep, the friend responded. Then the Chairwoman turned and looked at Quint, whose mouth was open in shock. Seeing this, she said matter-of-factly, 'Oh believe me, we know our men. I've been telling you that for years so you shouldn't be surprised. Right now, they're back there plotting how they're gonna go out without us.' They began to tell him the precise events that were about to take place. A short time later the husbands came into the kitchen. It was at this point Quint became a fly on the wall.

The first words out of the husband's mouths were exactly what The Chairwoman had said they would be. Needless to say, it worked out exactly as they'd explained it to him. In a short time the husbands were stuttering and stammering while trying to concoct a new plan. And, I might add, they were not doing a very good job of it. The room had become silent so Quint thought he would take this opportunity to leave. He figured the volume levels were about to rise and he didn't want to be there for that. During the drive home, he realized he could never win a war with women. And for the second time he gave in to serious thoughts of marriage.

When he talked to his lady about marriage, she told him he needed to exorcise the demons of his first relationship. She said if their marriage was going to get off to a good start he needed to know once and for all if he was over Love. The only way he could do it was to go see her. She said he if didn't do it he'd never be able to get into any relationship. It was really a brave thing for his lady to do. But I guess if you love someone enough, you're willing to let them go to be happy. He knew he still had feelings for Love, but until he faced her, any relationship he entered would be doomed from the start.

During the drive home, he thought about what his lady said. He realized she was right and, in the back of his mind, he'd always known this was something he'd eventually have to do. It was then he started the courage building process to go and face Love so he could finally get on with his life...

Some things you do for satisfaction,
Some things you do for fun.
Some things you do in desperation,
Some things because you must.
Twelve years to get the courage,
to get back to number one.
It was something I had to do,
so I could get on with my life,
and get it straight with you.
Twelve years of carrying torches,
Through love, hate, and reborn love,
though this she never knew.
Twelve years to get the courage,
to get it straight with you.
Through rebound love deceptions,
this torch I carried through.
Twelve years to get the courage,
to do what I had to do.
Some things you do for satisfaction,
Some things you do for fun,
Some things you do in desperation,
some things because you must.
I finally got the courage,
to do what I had to do.
To get on with my life,
and get it straight with you..."

Chapter 17

Exorcising Demons

Falling twelve years hard, recovering in never. True love is not a faucet, can't turn it off and on. For it will still be living, when eternity is gone. Falling twelve years hard, recovering in never.

The Reunion

"Early in the year Quint contacted Love's brother; he worked in the area and got Love's phone number from him. After building up enough courage, he called her in early May and made an appointment to see her. Later that month, he saw her for the first time since their November meeting of four years before.

During the nearly four hour drive to her place he went over all the things that had happened to him after she left. Through it all he had some regrets, but he felt he'd come out okay. The only lingering regret was Jen, for he was still having a problem with the way he left her. The other thing he kept reminding himself was not to look into Love's eyes too often or too long because he knew what they could do to him. When he neared her home, he stopped at a florist and bought two flowers wrapped separately. Pulling into her parking lot he thought, for a fleeting second, he should abandon the whole idea. But he had come too far and the real reason he came was never going to be resolved if he gave up now. As he walked up to her townhouse and rang the bell he told himself again to avoid looking too long at her eyes. He knew he was about to face the moment of truth.

She answered the door wearing all red. When he saw her, he was both happy and apprehensive but, as usual, she made him feel comfortable. At that time she was separated from her husband who was living on the West Coast. She was more beautiful now than she had ever been and the second he saw her he knew he could have loved her forever. It wasn't the passionate emotion it had once been; it was now a love rooted in their past at a time of innocence. Since they couldn't go back there again, it would have to be just a fond memory. After all, she was his lady of firsts and you never forget the firsts.

"She introduced him to her daughter and he gave each of them a flower. They sat on the sofa and started catching up on twelve years of missed conversation. The whole time her daughter was sitting right next to her mother and he could see the love she had for this child.

You wear your love so sweetly, It fits your soul so nice.
It's loose about the shoulders, And snugs your heart so tight.

You wear your love so sweetly, In shades of every hue, Eyes sparkle when you're happy, A muted smile when blue.

You wear your love so neatly, It's striking and it's bold, Yet fits your shape uniquely, From follicle to sole.

You wear your love so chicly, In shades of every hue.
You wear your love uniquely, Because your love is you " .

After about an hour she told him her sisters wanted to see him. He drove them to the first sister's house. When they arrived, memories flooded back to him and after awhile it was like he'd never left. A short time later they left for another one of her sisters.

During the forty minute drive she told him he was the only former boyfriend that hadn't kept in touch and she wanted to know why. He told her he had loved her too much, and then he told her his story as she listened in silence. She was where his story had started and it was where it was going to have to begin again if he was going to be able to get on with his life. Now that he had made a commitment to his lady woman, he was going to keep it. Finally, he was going to have to make peace with the one woman he found irresistible. After this, the mood got lighter and she reminded him of the time he threw the milkhake in her face.

A Milkshake In The Face

'The events that led to this were now fuzzy in his mind. Like most people who have close relationships, when you get to know each other, you know which buttons to push in order to irritate the other person. Love was pushing these buttons with him one Saturday afternoon and she kept it up to the point he got so angry he wanted to hit her. Remembering what his Grandmother had taught him, he knew real men did not hit women. He continued to get angry so he left the house so he could calm down. He walked over to the local ice cream parlor, bought a chocolate milkshake and walked back to her house. When he got back he thought he had calmed down. He rang the bell and when she answered the door and he saw her, he got angry again. Since he could not hit her he did the only thing he could, he threw the milkshake in her face. He drove home feeling sorry the entire trip. When he got home he called her and apologized. They laughed about it later but, she never let him live it down.

They were pulling into her sister's driveway as they finished laughing about the milkshake incident. Again, seeing Love's sister brought back fond memories. They visited awhile and as they were leaving, he invited Love and her daughter to dinner at a Chinese restaurant. During dinner, questions and answers were flying back and forth so fast her daughter asked why she was asking him so many questions? She explained to her that they hadn't seen each other for a long time. After a lot of conversation and good food and laughter, they went back to her house.

It was rather late when they arrived and Love said she had to put her daughter to bed. While she was doing this, Quint was going through the all the things that had happened that the afternoon. Yes, she still turned him on. And yes, if he wasn't careful, he could still be passionately in love with her. He made a mental note not to look too long into her eyes. When she was finished putting her child in bed, she returned to the sofa and they continued the conversation.

By now they had covered most of the past events and were talking about the things they were now doing. He told her that he was about to get his license to be a masseuse. All of a sudden, she asked if he would give her a massage. He asked if she was sure and she said yes. She went to get some towels while he went out to the car to get his oils and the tape he used when giving massages.

When he returned, he put one of the towels on the living room floor and asked her to go in the other room, remove her clothes and put a towel around her. Since he knew she would be asleep when he finished, he asked her how to lock the door when he left. Now if a full body massage is done properly it should take about ninety minutes, which is exactly how long his tape was. He prepared his hands and put on dual headphones, one on her and one for him, and started the massage. Listening to Lonnie Listen Smith was ninety minutes of concentration and sweat which left him with a raging lust. After he finished, Love was asleep on the living room floor and he was determined not to wake her. Making sure that the door was locked, he left. He called her the next day before he left for home and they said good-bye.

He had won the most important battle of his life, the battle with himself. The massage session was a test for him. Love was the only woman he'd ever met whose body he couldn't resist He had his hands on her naked body for an hour and half and he passed the test with flying colors. He was now fully healed and committed to marry a wonderful woman. Thinking back about the events of that day and the things that were said in later conversations, he was now sure she didn't believe him when he told her about studying for his license. He later found out she wanted him to make love to her. Indeed, there were many things about the events of that day which indicated she'd had other intentions, including the red outfit (she knew he loved red). He didn't believe these intentions were premeditated but developed as the evening progressed. In all honesty, he really wanted her too. It had been a wonderful day and he had passed the most difficult test of his life. They continued to see each other at least once a year. Even though he still loved her, he could now deal with it maturely. Love always told her sisters that Quint blamed her for all the rotten things that happened to him after she left and he felt she held some guilt about this, which was later confirmed. "

Chapter 18

To Marriage And Beyond

It was now dark and the sky was full stars. It was eerily strange to be sitting there in the dark listening to Uncle Question's voice coming out of the darkness. He continued the story, "You know some women are like bears, in that they mark their perceived territory like a bear marks trees. Any young man that brings a female companion to his place would be well advised to check his place very carefully when they depart. Some women will leave objects around your place to mark the territory. As Quint was naive in such matters, he never noticed any of this. It would appear the more they're into you the more valuable the objects they leave. They do this for two reasons. To warn any other female that might happen to come over, and to have a reason to come back. As I said, Quint was naive to this until the day his now fiancée and The Chairwoman volunteered to clean his apartment."

The Cleaning

"It was a Saturday morning when they came over to clean his apartment. They never said anything to him about the objects they found. As they found them they would put them on the counter between his kitchen and dining area. Soon there was quite a collection of hairpins, earrings and even rings. More games he thought to himself as he threw them in the garbage can. He was throwing out a part of his life that he wouldn't miss. He thought any woman who would put up with this and all the other things he'd put her through must really love him. And he was glad he had asked her to marry him She never tried to change him She accepted him the way he was, just a man. Which reminds me about the first time he asked her to marry him.

This was after she had caught him in an attempted juggle. Afterward this he asked her to marry him the first time. A nanosecond after the words came from his mouth, the little voice in his head said, 'Fool what did you just do?' It must have showed on his face for she said to him, 'Are you sure about this?' He quickly retracted the statement saying he needed a little more time. A month or so later he asked her again but this time he meant it. When she accepted he went to her parents to ask permission to marry their daughter, and they gave him their blessing.

The Bachelor Party

Quint's bachelor party may have been one of the strangest ever. It was attended by a few of his male friends and The Committee minus The Chairwoman and of course the bride-to be. The drinks flowed and in no time he was near his limit. He was sitting at the bar with the Committee Member that he'd had those wild fantasies about. He told her, he always wanted to get it on with her. She looked at him and said, 'If that's what you wanted all you had to do was ask. But it's too late now, so don't even think about it.' Quint was flabbergasted. After all those years of the wildest fantasies you could imagine, all he had to do was ask. (Go figure) The rest of the night was a blur, and he got home at four in the morning. He got up at seven to tape the music for the wedding reception."

The Wedding

The best man picked him up when it was time to go to the church. The last thing he picked up before leaving the apartment was a small hand towel He had never been so terrified in all his life because marriage was supposed to be forever and that was a long time. When they got to the church he nearly panicked. It was that towel that saved the wedding. All he could think about was getting out of there. The best man, who was married, talked him out of leaving, and he twisted that towel almost in half All I can tell you about the wedding was the bride and groom were so nervous during the ceremony that they were leaning on each other for support. And they've been leaning on each other ever since.

The reception went about like all receptions go, with lots of family and friends having a good time. He was happy to see Love, her husband and several of her sisters make it. Love was trying to reconcile her relationship and it must have worked because she later had twins. Quint didn't see her for a while, as he was trying to adjust to his new married life."

Grandpa who hadn't said very much, spoke, "Getting married is the easy part. Staying married is the hard part. It requires a lot of patience, understanding and communication. As long as you can talk you always have a chance to make it. You are going to have good times and you are going to have some tough times. As long as you put your faith in God and your wife who should be your best friend, you'll do okay. There're times when you will be strong and other times when she will be strong. People are creatures of habit; sometimes folks get caught up in always having to be the strongest every time. Everybody is not going to be strong all the time. And when you're not, you need to be able to lean on your partner and Friend...

Lord grant me strength to show her strength when she is weak, and grant her strength to show me strength when I am weak.

"At some point you are going to be tempted and it is during these times you need to remember a moments fun isn't worth all you stand to lose. You always hear folks talk about working at a marriage. I've always thought it meant keeping the boredom out of it. And yes, there are times when a marriage gets boring. But don't ever wait on her to change things. You did things to make her love you in the first place and you should never forget what those things are. You've gotta continue to do them. If you do those things, she'll do the things that made you love her. If a man's handling his business, he won't have time to cheat. And don't put your woman on a pedestal in the bedroom. A lot of men would be surprised to discover their women are willing to try their freaky little fantasies. And you gotta be able to talk about it. So if you gotta cheat, be discreet. Remember in this family if you can cheat she can cheat, and divorce ain't an option."

Uncle Question continued the story saying, "Now Quint settled into married life pretty well. He'd passed seven years without the itch thinking it was a lot of crap. He'd long since renewed his friendship with Love and they saw each other pretty regularly over the years. By now Love was going through a messy divorce and now had three kids. During their get-togethers they'd talk about general subjects. On days she felt good she'd say him, 'I should have married you.' To which he'd respond, 'It wouldn't have worked.' When she'd ask why, he'd tell her she liked challenges and he was too easy going to challenge her. On the days she wasn't having a good day she'd say, 'I hate men.' To which Quint would ask,

'Does that include me?' She always told him she'd make an exception in his case.

"Quint knew his limitations and he continued to avoid long eye contacts with her. He also tried to avoid one-on-one situations. Usually there was someone else around so it wasn't a problem. They never went out together which made it easy for him to avoid any entanglements. One day they were sitting in her kitchen talking and she caught him looking at the counter. Out of the blue she asked him if he still liked her eyes? His answer to her was, 'No Question.' Then she asked why he never looked at them? He told her that he was still afraid of what they could do to him. She didn't say anything; she just smiled and sort of drifted off into a distant memory of her own, and never pressed the issue again til their last date.

"Love's eyes could reach his soul and he knew it. During their early years together he had spent hours looking into those eyes, and he knew what they could do to him. (Like Dirty Harry says, 'A man has got to know his limitations). At that moment all the things that had happened to him came flooding back. He was now married to the best wife any man could have, and he wasn't about to mess that up by looking into a pair of beautiful eyes. He was still deep in these thoughts when the first lyrics to' a song came to him. During his drive home this song continued to grow. By the time he got home a good piece of the song was done." Uncle Question then started singing...

If it hadn't been for that war, you know I never would have spoke to her Didn't have the confidence, and beauties don't go out with squares But through a letter introduced to me, was awful nice at least she seemed to be And I was just so ever young and prime, not ready for that fatal surprise

If it hadn't been for that war, you know I never would have spoke to her Didn't have the confidence, but through the letters became friends And then that picture she sent to me, oh my what do I see Oh Lord those great big thighs, but I got hooked on emerald eyes

Back home from the war in the world, you know I just had to see that girl Tiny waist and that beautify I smile, but I got hooked on emerald eyes From South Carolina in a geechie patch, Walterboro to be exact, Lord knows I never will go back, they caught me good on emerald eyes

Twelve years to get it straight, through the pain, and recovered hate Oh Lord what a cruel cruel fate, to get me hooked on emerald eyes This ain't no way to do Lillie's boy, take his heart and flyaway And what could Langhom say, Grandbaby's caught on emerald eyes

Twelve years to get it straight, through the pain and recovered hate Oh Lord what a cruel cruel fate, to get me caught on emerald eyes This ain't no way to do Lillie's boy, take his soul and flyaway And what could Langhom say, Grandbaby's caught on emerald eyes

Twelve years to get it straight, through the pain and recovered hate Oh Lord what a cruel cruel fate to get me hooked on emerald eyes And now I real-o-lize, I'm gonna love them 'til the day I die Tiny waist and I loved that style but I was caught on emerald eyes

Be ever loving emerald eyes, Those ever living emerald eyes I'll be loving emerald eyes...

"It was about this time the nature of Quint's job changed, and he was now required to travel more. The hub of his travel put him in close proximity to Love. She had moved into a beautiful new home and he'd built some furniture for one of her children's rooms. He avoided her as much as possible and when he was in the area he'd call her relatives. Occasionally he'd call her, or stop by and see her, but generally he avoided her as much as possible. He'd been in the area for a week-long workshop, and when it was over he called her. It had been a very good and emotional seminar and he was in a good mood. When she came to the phone she lit in to him. She wanted to know why he always called or visited her relatives but he didn't do the same thing with her. Then she told him she didn't bite and asked him if he was afraid of her? He said he wasn't and to prove it he was going to take her to dinner and. a movie."

The Last Date

"Quint had reservations about going out with her in a one-on-one situation. He knew if he allowed himself, he could love her and he wasn't sure how he'd react in this situation. As you will see, his trepidation was well founded. The night he picked her up was one of the most beautiful and romantic any man could have wished for. Here he was, a happily married man going out with this beautiful woman whom he had once loved so passionately. There was a full moon and she was looking especially sexy. During the trip to the restaurant they had a serious conversation about the things going on in theirs lives. She told him her life had gotten too complicated and she needed to slow it down. He told her to, 'keep every promise she made and she would make less promises and her life would get simpler.' Then they talked about the things they'd avoided talking about for years.

She asked why he hadn't come to California to get her after the break up? And he told her he'd been devastated after she left, and didn't think it would have done any good. She got misty eyed and said, 'You're the only man who ever really cared about me; I should have married you.' Her mood changed and she asked, 'Why didn't you make love to me at our reunion? You know that's what I wanted. Why did you put me to sleep and then leave?' This question really floored Quint and he had to think about the answer. He told her he'd made a commitment to the bride-to-be which he didn't take lightly. He also told he didn't know that's what she wanted. If she'd said so it might have happened. Now here they were on this beautiful romantic moonlit night having the conversation they'd avoided for nine years. And by now they were getting to the restaurant.

Lewis Wiyd

"Once inside they were seated in a private area with a glass ceiling which allowed a view of the full moon. They ordered a bottle of wine and during dinner the conversation got sexually provocative, and. they were getting very turned on. He made the mistake of talking long looks into her beautiful green eyes which was a taboo for him. You know, trying to relive the past can be a very dangerous thing. When the waitress came to offer the dessert, Quint told her he'd have the lady for dessert. The waitress blushed, but at that moment he was dead serious. He'd all but forgotten he was married. But you know God takes care of fools and babies, and in this case He provided the universal healer, time. When they got outside after dinner and the cool evening air hit Quint in the face, he started having fears and regrets.

During the drive to the theater and all through the movie, 'Boomerang' he kept thinking to himself that he had let his mouth write checks his conscience couldn't cash. He was struggling to figure out a graceful way to get out of this situation, save face and not appear to be either a fool or a tease. "Now he had been a happily married man for years, and this was the first time before or since that he'd been even remotely tempted into an act of infidelity. Fortunately, fate and the length of the movie were long enough for them to both cool down. After the movie, he took her home and she rang the bell and her daughter opened the door. He kissed her on the cheek and thanked her for a wonderful evening. On the way home, He relived the events the evening, and he realized that Love was the only woman who could have ever put him in this position. When he got to where he was staying he wrote her a poem, which he intended to drop off the following day on his way home.

The next day he called to find out if it would be okay to stop by her house to drop off the poem When she answered the phone Quint greeted her with, 'Good morning, sexy.' She told him she wasn't feeling very sexy. During the drive to her house, he relived the events of the previous night He vowed he'd never let it happen again. Love had had a fight with her ex-husband and wasn't in a very good mood. But when she read the poem he gave her, she gave him a hug and he left...

It could have been the setting,
or maybe just white wine.
But you really are amazing,
in fact it blows my mind.
This power you have to turn me on,
even after all this time.
I thought I knew my limitations,
and to everyone could shout.
But during the pleasant dining,
there creeps in room for doubt.
And this thing that I first loved in you,
and later to despise.
The power they still hold on me,
your beautiful green eyes.
Or explicit, steamy conversation
to make the passion swoon.
It might have been nothing more,
than the clouded yellow moon.
Maybe any one of these things, or all three in concert.
But I voiced aloud to the waitress,
that I'd have you for dessert.
And maybe curiosity of time and space,
conspire to break a trust.
Or it could have been just nothing more,
than pure unbridled lust...

Lewis Wiyd

There was no way he could ever know as he left her house this would be the last time he would ever see her again. Seven months after their last date he lost her tragically. There had been an empty feeling in him for several days and he didn't know why. He'd worked through his regular lunch period and was home having a late lunch when the call came that she was dead.

"He wasn't able to make the funeral, but several hundred people attended. He secretly grieved for three years. He never realized what an effect Love had on his life until she wasn't there. Society does men a great disservice by saying men aren't supposed to cry. I think it's the reason women out live men is they're allowed to show emotions. Men carry around emotional baggage which eventually kills them. Junior, I want you to remember, if something hurts emotionally it's often more painful than a physical injury. It takes longer to heal, so if it hurts, you let it out and move on with your life. Quint carried his grief buried deep within. Love represented the springtime of his life and there was a void which couldn't be filled. He held in the grief until the spring of the third year when it boiled over and he cried. There was no closure until he put his grief on paper...

Speak not to me of my successes,
For 'tis love's failures for which I grieve.
I've felt the jagged sting of lost love pain,
and cried through nights to question why.
Have felt the singe of burning words,
"We need to consider our relationship...
or, perhaps we should just be friends."
Losing confidence from having love's rug
pulled from beneath the feet of my heart.
Moving on to hate, lashing out with anger,

Healing through time; feeling the sharp pain
become the dull ache of a fond memory.
Do not speak to me of the good,
or the positive things I have done
For 'tis love's failures for which I grieve"

It was the strangest and thing I'd ever experienced. Uncle Question's voice in the darkness poring out his heart and I could feel the pain and loss. We lapsed into another of those silences which lasted for some time before out of the darkness Dad said, "Everything about love isn't sad; there can be a lot of comedy too. Take for example every time your mom and I go out...

Let me tell you what's most unfair
Every time we're gettin' ready to go somewhere
I know the very first thing I'm gonna hear,
I ain't got nothin' to wear

The house has six closets and I got one,
and let me tell you now, it sure ain't fun
'cause every time we gotta go somewhere
I know the first thing I'm gonna hear
I ain't got nothin' to wear

She's got three big closets of real bad rags
and half of them still got on the tags
Yet every time we have to go somewhere
She's got nothing to wear

She done put on the makeup and combed her hair
Then she stands in three closets and tries to compare
And I know the very next thing that I'm gonna hear,

Lewis Wiyd

I ain't got nothin' to wear

Now this same old song is gettin to be a drag
'Cause she's got a closet for shoes and another for bags
Yet when it comes time to go somewhere,
She's got nothin' to wear

I came home one day and what did I find
She had the nerve to be moving her stuff into mine
But when it comes time for us to go somewhere
I know the first thing that I'm gonna hear, is
I ain't got nothin' to wear...

We all broke into laughter after this and when we had calmed down Dad said, "Being in a marriage can be a pattern of sameness and it can be both bad, and good. Most people are creatures of habit and resistant to change. But you must never let it get boring. You do this by continuing to grow as a person and if you have the right mate it will be a lifetime growing experience. As you grow individually, you also grow together and the bonds get deeper everyday. And never forget to tell your woman that you love her. It is the simplest of all things to do, but most often forgotten, but you're still a man and as such you will still be tempted, but like your Grandpa said you must always think about what you stand to lose. So always remember who is always in your corner and never take that for granted. During those times when you see a woman that gets your juices flowing you go back to the basic question is it love or is it lust.

When the juices start to flow you got to grab hold of passion's horses and take them back to your own barn. I say again never take anything for granted. If you do these things you will do well in whatever you do. A wife should be a source of inspiration to you everyday and when you get a good one, you thank God because now-a-days it's becoming increasingly rare to find one. So when you find a good one, never forget to tell her how much you love her.

Then Grandpa said, "You know Junior, one of the hardest concepts to learn in a relationship is space. You can suffocate a relationship by not allowing your partner the space they need to grow. That's where trust comes in. There's an old jazz song called *No Faith, No Love* and you have trust they'll do what's right. You can't second-guess them for a decision they've made during a critical situation. Your judgment is always made from twenty-twenty hindsight. And you couldn't know whether or not you'd have made the same decision given the information at hand. You gotta have faith in their decisions right or wrong and work together to fix any mistakes.

After a pause, he said, 'Well Junior, that's about all we can tell you. If you take heed to the things we've told you here, you'll do fine. And we know we can count on you to keep the family tradition going. As you've heard all your life there's never been a divorce in the Rhymes family. And now maybe you know why." Then Grandpa said a prayer and when he finished he asked me if I had any questions? So I asked the question that everybody has been asking since time began, I asked him, 'What is love?' He answered saying, "I don't rightly know what love is, but I know what love is not." He started singing, this bluesy number, as Dad and Uncle Question did the back ground harmonies...

Love don't promise no stars or moons
or no gold up in the sky.
Love don't ask no questions
and don't ever wonder why.

It never asks you where you been,
Or who you been there with.
For love is what it always is,
And in patience ever sits.
Love don't ever cause no pain,
and don't ever cause abuse.
Just put the blame on foolishness,
Don't use love as the excuse.
Love don't seek no fortune,
Love don't seek no fame.
Love don't make no babies,
But still love gets the blame.
For love is an emotion,
Sometimes cold and sometimes hot.
You might not know what love is,
But you know what love is not.
Been sitting there for eons,
and just goes on and on.
And it was here before you were,
and will be when you're gone.
Love is never selfish, and it will ever share,
Will lend it's self to anyone,
who has a heart that cares.
Love is not abusive, and it inflicts no pain.
Love don't make no babies,
But still love gets the blame.
For love is an emotion,
Sometimes cold and sometimes hot,
You might not know what love is,
But you know what love is not... "

When they'd finished, I had one last question for my Uncle. I asked him,. "What ever happened to Jen?" He said, "As it turned out, Jen landed firmly on her feet. I was thumbing through the pages of Black Enterprise one day and saw a picture of her. She owns an industrial design consulting firm with over fifty employees and she's doing quite well. In the long run, I would have been a liability for her. All things work out for a reason, though sometimes we don't know what the reason is. I liked her very much, but I respected her more, and her success removed some of my guilt. It won't however, remove the guilt about how I left her, but that was a lesson in honor I'll have to live with.

Then Grandpa said, "One last thing Junior, you remember to always keep a healthy respect for women. I know it's getting harder to do with all the role changes and such. And some of the women are now acting more like men. But you must remember a woman is one of the most sacred things God ever put on this earth. Although they committed the first sin, they also created civilization and should always be treated with reverence and respect for that reason alone."

When Grandpa finished he said, "Well it's getting late and I guess we should be getting in the house." At that moment Grandma turned on the porch light and said, 'Wisdom, don't you think you've been out there long enough? We've got to get ready for tomorrow." "We're comin in now Puddin," he said, as he got up from his rocking chair. I reached down and turned off my tape recorder that had mysteriously appeared before we came out onto the porch. I had a lot to think about and it was going to take some time to sort it out, but I now knew the family secret. The rest of the reunion went about as usual, and we left for home on Sunday.

Chapter 19

A Phone Call from Mom

A couple of days after we got home from the reunion I got a phone call from my Mom. My Mom is a great person and she's supported me in whatever I've ever done, no matter how crazy it was. Her only concern was always that I didn't get hurt. We can talk about anything and she has always guided me wisely. After a few minutes of idle chit chat she asked me, "How did the puppy do on the porch with the big dogs?" At first I had no idea what she was talking about. Then she said, "You know, the session with Grandpa, your Father and your Uncle on the porch at Grandpa's."

I immediately knew what she was talking about. And I told her that I had done okay. Then I told her I'd learned a lot from it. She said, "You know there's never been a divorce in the family. What you were involved in was a family tradition. It's called putting 'The Dogs On The Porch.' It is a Rite of Passage and it's a very serious matter in this family. Do you understand what I'm saying to you?" I told her I did and she could count on me to keep the tradition. Then she said, "Too many women out here today believe 'Men are dogs.' The real victims of this thinking are not the women, but men. They buy into it and think they should act like dogs in heat all the time. It shouldn't to be that way." Then she hung up, after which I pulled out the tapes of the session on Grandpa's porch. I listened to the whole thing again. And I now had a completely new view point to consider regarding the phrase, "All Men Are Dogs "